SAKAR

A SCI-FI HOLIDAY TAIL

STRANDED WITH AN ALIEN SERIES

ELLA BLAKE

SAKAR: A Sci-Fi Holiday Tail

Stranded with an Alien series

Copyright © 2022 Ella Blake

First edition: November 11, 2022

Stock Art: Depositphotos

Cover Design: Natasha Snow Designs

ALSO BY ELLA BLAKE

Stryxian Alien Warriors

BONDED TO THE STRYXIAN

STRANDED WITH THE STRYXIAN (free novella)

SAVED BY THE STRYXIAN

CLAIMED BY THE STRYXIAN

POSSESSED BY THE STRYXIAN

CHAINED TO THE STRYXIAN

SEDUCED BY THE STRYXIAN

Virilian Mail Order Mates

TRAK

DREX

VIRAK

NIIR

TARON

KIM & KLAE (novella)

SERIES BOX SET

SAKAR: A Sci-Fi Holiday Tail

The Baylan Chronicles

DRACE

RAZE

ARTEN

HARC

ZADE

The Lords of Destra

LOST TO THE ALIEN LORD

BOUND TO THE ALIEN LORD

FATED TO THE ALIEN LORD

CRAVED BY THE ALIEN LORD

DESTINED FOR THE ALIEN LORD

ENSNARED BY THE ALIEN LORD

This is a standalone story in the Virilian Mail Order Mates world and takes place after the events of the series.

My two girls and I are going to be snowed in for Christmas and that's fine with us, until an alien spacecraft crashes behind our wooded Maine home. I take the gorgeous Virilian, Prince Sakar, home with me. He's injured and tracking an endangered alien dog with a taste for my neighbor's goats. Spending Christmas with an alien prince is the last thing my daughters and I expected, next to my falling in love with him. My heart's been beaten up plenty, but can I take a chance on this male who adores my young girls and awakens desires I thought long dead?

I usually avoid Earth at all costs, but tracking the *daerli* led me to crash-landing on Nessa's property in the middle of a snowstorm. My kind are forbidden on Earth, but I can't leave without the rare creature I'm tracking, and the female I'm stranded with has enthralled me. I want her with all of my being. When the human authorities arrive to take me away, the deepest hidden side of my Virilian nature comes out to protect her. I must find a way to prove to Nessa that I am her fated mate, or lose her forever.

CHAPTER 1

Sakar

Bring him back alive.

The words from my king slid through my head as I flew my Endross-77 so close to my prey that I could all but smell the burn of their spent fuel cell. It was a chase I hadn't anticipated. The smugglers were transporting one of the last remaining *daerli* hounds to an unknown fate.

King Virak, leader of Tagja City on my home planet of Virilia, had a female *daerli* in his refuge. The one on the vessel I chased was male. My king wanted to keep the species alive by breeding them. So here I was, pushing my ship to its limits to intercept a Shaax vessel, retrieve the *daerli*, and return it to Virilia. *Alive.*

It hadn't seemed so hard when I started off. The Shaax were cowardly. I outgunned them and my ship could keep up with them. But because I was retrieving a living creature, there would be no blasting the ship to pieces and swinging back home.

To make things worse, we were in an off-limits planetary

system. I cursed, realizing where the Shaax smugglers were heading—directly toward a planet Virilians were not advised to go near without a pile of clearances and permits: Earth.

Ah, Earth. I had many feelings about this planet. All of them were conflicted. On one hand, the match program was a success so far and many Virilian males had found mates that had produced much-needed offspring. But humans were a difficult and cantankerous species to work with. Not to mention suspicious. They had to know that if we wanted to take over their planet, we could have done so a hundred times over. *But no.* They still made us fill out a staggering number of forms to even make contact with anyone on their planet.

My com system pinged. The Shaax captain's gurgling voice came over, translated by the language chip in my head. "Cease your pursuit, Virilian, or we will continue to Earth, where you are not welcome."

"You are not, either," I gritted back. "You will be attacked."

Laughter was the reply. "My ship can withstand anything those small creatures can send out."

"They are better equipped than you think."

"*You* cannot risk angering them," the captain taunted. "You need their females. We do not."

We were getting dangerously close to the range of Earth's satellites. "Agree to hand over the *daerli* and neither of us needs to risk our lives here."

A hissing sound grated over the com. "This beast is destined for the plate of High Warlord Woork for his nuptials to Princess Rankita. It was purchased fairly, at auction."

The *daerli* was meant to be *eaten?* The thought made my blood boil. "There is nothing fair about those auctions," I spat. "They're cruel and illegal and you know it. I will take that *daerli,* then gut you for my trouble."

That reply had been unwise. I realized it the moment the words left my mouth. I heard a growl over the com. "Have it your way, Virilian."

The Shaax headed straight for Earth. I cursed again, annoyed with myself, but knowing that all the diplomacy in the world wouldn't have changed the Shaax's course.

I reached for a metal case from one of the compartments in my control console. Muttering curses, I found what I was looking for. It was a tiny chip among a few dozen others. I felt through the hair at the base of my skull, took out the Shaax chip and inserted the English one into the slot there. I felt a wave of light-headedness as my brain accepted the new language. I would need to listen in on Earth's military's attempts to communicate. Language chips made it so much easier to deal with other species, even though the process of getting the neural port inserted in my head had been unpleasant.

The white clouds and blue seas of planet Earth were getting clearer. I could pull off, swing around and try to catch the Shaax when they were away from the planet, but their ship was as fast as mine and one incorrect move would put them out of my reach for good. Instead, I engaged my distortion field, which rendered my ship temporarily invisible to Earth's satellites.

I could see my coms lighting up in a brilliant display. The humans had picked up the Shaax ship speeding toward them and wanted an explanation. I already knew how this would go.

I opened the com link and prepared myself for the onslaught. At least four different humans started speaking at once—*state your purpose...choose a different course heading... reroute your path immediately...you'll be fired upon.* The Shaax ship was undoubtedly getting peppered with these communications too, but they had no knowledge of the humans' language and didn't care.

They *would* care when they were fired on, and they underestimated the strength of Earth's weaponry. I could say for a fact it was not as puny as the Shaax believed.

The flurry of incoming transmissions became almost incomprehensible as other languages joined in, turning it into a drone of noise. I turned off the coms and concentrated on the Shaax ship that was heading recklessly for the planet. I couldn't imagine what they were thinking. Were they that arrogant?

The shields hid my ship, which was a newer model with a very high cloak rating. I braced for some of the shots to hit me, just because of proximity. I worried about the *daerli* trapped in the Shaax ship. If the humans managed to destroy it, there would be one less specimen to restore the species to Virilia.

My onboard surveillance system tracked incoming missiles and they were headed in the Shaax's direction. I maneuvered to dodge them. After several hits, smoke streamed from the Shaax's hull. They were going down. I would follow them, retrieve the *daerli* and leave before the humans even knew I was there.

I set my scanner to track the Shaax ship as it hurtled toward the surface. The temperature rose as my ship moved through the atmosphere. The data screen displayed the standard warnings about heat, speed, and pressure. I wasn't worried. My ship would hold. Hopefully, the Shaax ship would, too.

Just as I thought I was in the clear, the Shaax ship released a barrage of pulse waves designed to disable the controls of a ship in close pursuit. I *didn't* expect this. Stuck on the trajectory I was on, I couldn't navigate. I still had my distortion field—barely—so I was still evading the humans' scanners, but we were going down—both of us. The Shaax ship and mine.

My hands flew over the controls, desperate to stabilize my ship and keep it from crashing. I could still land it, awkwardly, if I could find a safe place to bring it down. Hopefully, it wouldn't be in a city or densely occupied area. And preferably not in a body of water. My ship wasn't designed for that.

I kept my lock on the Shaax ship and let out a breath of relief as I watched a thickly forested area rush up toward us. With luck, there would be no people nearby. More than likely the *daerli* was kept in a containment unit on board the Shaax ship. I'd get down there, bring the *daerli* onto my ship, run the self-repair program and get out as quickly as possible.

The humans wouldn't even know I was here. Then, they could pick apart the Shaax ship and be pleased that they successfully stopped an alien from landing on their planet. Everyone would win. The *daerli* would be spared the fate of a warlord's nuptial dinner, and instead meet a lovely female of his own species.

And I would never have to come near this planet again. Humans were just too unpredictable and warlike for my taste.

CHAPTER 2

Nessa

"**M**om, what was that crash?"

"*What* crash?" I pulled the headset off my ears and peered at the eight- and eleven-year-old girls standing there, gazing at me.

Violet, my older daughter, blinked and pointed at the window. "It sounded like something exploded in the woods."

"Exploded?" This was either a really bad thing or a gross exaggeration. Either was possible with these two. I got up and peered outside. In the distance, but not *enough* of a distance for my comfort, a trail of smoke curled up through the thick trees. My family had owned the two hundred acres I'd grown up on for four generations. As far as I knew, nothing had blown up on them, aside from my father's Buick that one time.

The first flakes of what the weather forecasters predicted would be an epic storm, were falling. I let out a string of curse words—only in my head, unfortunately—and went to grab my coat and boots.

"What do you think it is?" Violet asked anxiously. She tended to be my worrier. "Maybe it's a meteor."

"Maybe it was a *bomb*," said Mia, who usually went for the most apocalyptic scenario.

"Maybe somebody crashed their drone," I said.

"It was too loud to be a drone crashing," Violet said immediately. "You didn't hear it?"

"No. I was working with my headphones on." I had about a half dozen ways I made ends meet, living in a rural area of Maine. Medical transcription was one of them, along with selling apples from our orchard in the fall and maple syrup in the early spring. The transcription gave me a fairly flexible schedule, though, so I could deal with things that came up, like shit exploding in my woods.

"What if it was an airplane?" said Violet.

I paused with my hands halfway in my gloves. Now *that* was an actual possibility. "I certainly hope not," I said, suddenly more than a little terrified about what I might find out there.

I pulled on my fur-lined bomber hat and tucked my cell phone in the pocket of my down coat. "You two stay in the house. I'll be back shortly."

I trudged out into the snow. It was December twenty-third. The kids were on Christmas vacation. We were going to be snowed in for the holidays, and that was all right with the three of us. We'd stocked up on wood for the stove, books, and lots of food. But someone could be hurt out there —or worse.

I didn't know who or what I'd encounter out there, so I put my shotgun on the floor of the UTV, which was indispensable during apple and syrup seasons. It had four seats, a cranky starter, and guzzled gas like water. We all lovingly called it "Belcher." It handled the snowy terrain quite well.

Belcher started up when I turned the key. The two cows

that lived in the barn, mooed reproachfully at the sound and puff of exhaust. The horse, Prince Charming, who did *not* live up to his name, barely glanced up from his feed. The chickens were all outside, enjoying this little bit of time in the fresh air before the storm came.

I eased Belcher out of the barn and toward the wide trail that led into the wooded acres of my property. It *was* my property; I was still trying to remember that. My parents passed two years ago, the same year as my divorce.

Belcher made short work of the trails. Under different circumstances, it was fun to race this thing through the woods. It was bouncy and loud, but the girls squealed with delight whenever we did this.

Off the main trail, it was even more bouncy as I maneuvered over rocks and roots, around trees and up and down over the uneven ground. Belcher didn't have a windshield, but did have a robust metal frame around the seating area, which kept the big branches from whacking me in the face. I followed the smell of smoke and the thickening air as I got closer to the impact site.

My belly clenched at the thought of what I might find there. Would it be a small airplane with bodies strewn about? Would someone need help? I was no paramedic, but I would do what I could and call for help. Or would I find a bunch of assholes setting off explosives for fun in the woods? That was the reason I'd brought the shotgun. It wouldn't be the first time I found drunk guys being stupid on my property. There was an old hunting cabin somewhere out here that I cleaned beer cans out of a few times a year.

I knew I was close when the air turned acutely acrid and dense with smoke. I slowed down. It was hard to see here, between the smoke and the snow. But I knew these woods like the beating of my own heart.

I spotted a clearing that hadn't been here before. Something large had gone down. Sweat chilled on my spine. I eased Belcher around uprooted trees and flattened ground. I stopped the vehicle and turned it off. There was silence, except for the licking crackle of flames.

I couldn't breathe, and it wasn't because of the air quality. This wasn't the work of local kids up to nonsense in the woods. But it also wasn't an airplane. No, this wasn't anything that belonged in this world.

* * *

THERE WERE *two* spacecrafts crashed in my forest. One looked intact, but had landed awkwardly. It was roughly the size of a school bus, was sleek metal and teardrop shaped, blackened in areas and sporting a few nice dents where it'd crash-landed. The other ship was obliterated. I was no expert in alien space wrecks, but the second ship appeared to have been blasted apart, rather than crashed. There was no way of even telling what it looked like before, when it was intact.

Together, the ships had flattened about a half-acre strip of land. A quick glance at the fires reassured me that the woods would not be catching. They were small and already ebbing, as the ships cooled in the snowy, cold Maine winter.

My attention slid from the ships to a movement on the ground. An alien lay there. I'd never seen aliens like this before. It was a short, stocky being, with thick, trunk-like legs. It appeared to have a hunched back and claws on the end of three-fingered hands. It stretched out an arm, let out a croaking sound, then lay still. Large, sightless eyes and gray skin cooled in the freezing air.

I let out a whimper as I took in the whole scene. Maybe my mind had blocked it out at first, but now I saw, to my horror, that I'd stepped into a full, horrific crash site. There were more dead aliens on the ground—five, that I could see. The twisted metal of the wreck could hold more bodies.

I just gaped. I had no idea what to do. This was a total Roswell moment, but these days, we *knew* that aliens were real and visited Earth. We had women who were married to them. This wasn't shocking to me. The bodies *were*. Seeing the burning ship and smelling the smoke that made my eyes water and put a bitter taste in my mouth was more than shocking. It was horrifying.

A twisted hunk of metal moved. The wrecked spacecraft had a survivor, it seemed. Something was trapped and trying to free itself. Should I free the trapped…*thing?* It was possible the alien under the metal was as peaceful as could be, but it could also charge out and kill me. I didn't know.

I just stood there with my shotgun, about as effective as a stuffed animal, my blood pounding so hard it sounded like a drum in my head. The thing behind the metal was making progress. I backed up shakily. My breathing was shallow. Suddenly, the metal piece flew off and a creature leaped from the smoldering wreckage.

It was a dog in that it had four legs and a snout, but that was where the similarities ended. This thing was the size of a small horse. It had a set of horns that curled away from its head and down either side of its jaw. Huge fangs shot up from its lower jaw and slitted black eyes gazed out. It had a thick pelt of black fur that was burned off in some places, revealing red, raw skin. Smoke curled off its singed coat. A tight metal collar was around its neck. Stringy drool swung from its mouth. Instead of dog paws, its feet were almost like hands, complete with long claw-tipped toes.

It shook its body and blinked as if disoriented, but then its gaze turned to me. It bared its huge teeth in the most horrifying snarl I'd ever seen. My shotgun felt like it weighed a thousand pounds as I tried to lift it and turn off the safety.

My arms trembled so badly, they were like rubber. Never mind the fact that the only living thing I'd ever shot with this gun was a rabid raccoon, I'd never seen anything like this creature and it terrified me to my core.

The doglike thing lowered its head and took a step toward me.

Suddenly, the hatch on the other, intact spaceship—which I'd half forgotten about—flew open and another being stepped out. This was a Virilian. I knew what they looked like well enough—tall, powerful, with a blue, barbed-tipped tail. I felt a wave of relief. These beings were considered our allies, sort of.

Humans and Virilians had a mail-order bride/baby-making situation going on. They had very few females, were in danger of their species dying out, and we, well, frankly, we had more women than men. Any woman of childbearing age could sign up for the Virilian match program. If she was chosen, she could try to land herself an alien husband. It had worked out really well for a number of women. They needed babies, even human-Virilian hybrid ones, and we were a compatible species. The initial rules were simple—produce a child with a Virilian male. If she did, she could stay on Virilia with the male and the child, or leave the child with their father and return to Earth a very, *very* rich woman. Some didn't choose to stay there, but more and more did.

I'd even mused about it, but never seriously. I had two wonderful children and knew I could never walk away from a third. Besides, I was forty, and that was probably too old for the match program. Forty was apparently too old for a lot of things, according to the internet. It was definitely too old to be dealing with an alien ship crash in my backyard. I shoved away my fear, got my head together, and lifted my shotgun.

The alien dog swung its attention to the Virilian male, whose tail swished back and forth like an agitated cat.

Oh my. Words came to mind—tall, male, breathtakingly powerful. He wore dark brown leather pants that fit him like a second skin, showing the thickly muscled thighs and the large bulge of his package. Sturdy boots came up almost to his knees. He wore nothing from the waist up. Dozens of metal and leather bracelets collected on his wrists. Light brown hair, streaked with blond, came to his shoulders. His skin was golden and swirled with blue-gray markings.

The male held up a hand toward me, then brought it down, silently asking me to lower my weapon, but forget that. I was maybe twenty feet from an alien creature who could fit my whole head inside its mouth.

The Virilian turned his attention to the beast. He held up his hands in a calming gesture and took a step forward. He spoke in a soothing voice, using words I didn't know. His movements were slow and he bent over a little bit.

The creature turned its head, shifting its attention from me to the Virilian. I stared in confusion. Was he *trying* to get himself killed? But the way he spoke and the gestures he used had an effect on it. The giant dog thing cocked its head like a retriever and blinked its narrow black eyes.

For a moment, it looked as though he had calmed this creature. It took a step toward the Virilian. It stretched its neck and shook its head again, making it look as if the collar was bothering it. Whatever the Virilian was saying to it, the alien dog was responding.

I let the shotgun muzzle drift downward. This Virilian had just *saved my life*. He was only a few feet from this beast and showed no fear of it. He reached toward it as if he *wanted* to touch it, making him either very foolish or incredibly brave. His hand found the metal collar and depressed something, which made it unclasp and fall off. The creature shook its head again and let out a soft, crooning sound.

The Virilian smiled. His stance relaxed, but just as his hands were about to touch that thick black fur, something from the mangled parts of the destroyed ship exploded, sending burning scraps of metal up in an arc.

I yelped and jumped aside as a chunk of debris landed beside me. The explosion was enough to startle the beast and break the spell the Virilian had over it. The alien dog turned away, let out a garbled howl, and leaped over the debris. It streaked into the woods and disappeared.

CHAPTER 3

Nessa

"What the hell was that?" I put the safety back on the shotgun and pointed in the direction the alien dog took off in. "What happened here?" I didn't expect answers. Virilians didn't speak my language and he wasn't paying attention to me anyway. He rested his hands on his thighs and lowered his head, looking defeated.

With shaky hands, I took out my cell phone. I *knew* I had coverage out here. "Fuck this. I'm calling NASA. The Department of Planetary…something. I don't know. *Somebody.*"

But when I unlocked my phone, the screen blinked off. I smacked it against my palm, because that *always* works, closed the phone app, then opened it again. Nothing. I gave the ship a hard look. Something in it must be affecting my electronics.

"Do not summon the authorities," said the Virilian in a deep growly voice.

He spoke my language. That would make things easier. "Why not?"

"I am Prince Sakar Braal and that creature must be protected." He looked around, eyes going keen and sharp in the woods around us. "What lies in that direction, human?"

"Woods," I replied, trying not to be annoyed at being called "human" in a dismissive tone, and barely registering the "Prince" part of his name. "*My* woods, for about forty acres, then it turns into Martha Davidson's woods. What did you do to my phone?" I asked. "And why shouldn't I call the authorities, *Virilian?*"

He looked up at me. Muscles bulged as he rose to his full height. "I did nothing to your device." He blinked, then staggered a few steps. "I was pursuing a ship carrying a rare creature."

"That thing?" I pointed in the direction the alien dog had bolted.

"Yes," he said. "The creature is a male *daerli*, and if you call your people, they will hunt him and he will be killed."

"How is that my problem?" My back, beneath my heavy coat, was soaked with sweat. I wasn't feeling terribly sympathetic toward the *daerli* that looked like it had seen me as an afternoon snack.

"He is one of the last of his kind," Sakar said in a quiet voice, filled with the sympathy I lacked. "King Virak of Tagja City in Virilia has a female to match with him. They are native to Virilia, or, they were, long ago. We are trying to save their species."

"What about these?" I asked, gesturing to the dead aliens. "Did you shoot their ship down to 'save' these *daerli* creatures?"

"I did not," he said, offended. "The Shaax scum I chased here were delivering the *daerli* to his death. He was to be served at a warlord's wedding feast. It was your people who fired upon the Shaax ship, not I."

I stared at him, watching what little energy he had left drain away. His shoulders rounded and his face paled.

His very *handsome* face. I'd followed the Virilian match story just like everyone else these last few years, but not as closely as some. I'd been too busy raising my two girls, getting divorced, and taking care of my parents as they declined and passed. The story had been an interesting diversion, but the alien fervor that had gripped the world had been as real to me as a Hollywood drama.

But here was one of them, standing right in front of me. They weren't kidding about the Virilians' attractiveness. This guy was overwhelmingly good-looking. He had a weathered look about him, which made me think he was older than I was. He bore the signature black skin around his eyes, which made all Virilians look as though they wore smudged black eyeliner all the time. It was just the way they looked, but it made this male's light blue eyes almost glow from the contrast.

He staggered a few steps. "Do what you want, human," he said with a sigh. "I cannot stop you. I did not endure my own crash unscathed."

"My name isn't Human. It's Nessa Thompson," I said and laid my shotgun on the ground. "You better sit down or you're going to fall over."

He shook his head. "I need to find the *daerli* before…" He dropped to one knee. His hand went to his head where a deep purple bruise spread from his hairline onto his forehead.

"Oh, no you don't." I braced my shoulder under the large Virilian male's and took on some of his unsteady weight. He loomed over me. He had to be six-foot-five *at least*. And if I didn't get him in my vehicle, he was going to keel over and pass out. I'd never be able to help him, then.

And I *was* going to help him. That animal was going to

attack me and he was the reason it didn't. I owed him one. I looked up at the sky, which was silver gray and heavy. The snow was increasing. "I'm getting you back to the house before you pass out. We'll talk about your alien dog later."

Relief passed over his handsome features. A huge, warm hand wrapped around my shoulder and engulfed the entire joint. A jolt of...something zoomed through me like a light, electrical current. I pressed my lips together, almost able to taste the flavor of his touch. "My ship..."

"Right. How badly is it damaged?" I asked.

"Not terribly, I believe, but I cannot operate it in my condition. I am seeing two of everything."

I winced. "We are getting a monster storm tonight. Your ship will have to wait, but..." I looked at the dead aliens who lay on the ground. A fine layer of snow had fallen on them, coating them in glittering white. "What about these?"

He peeled back his lips to reveal longer, pointed canine teeth. "The Shaax can rot there for all I care."

I needed alien corpses on my property like I needed a hole in the head, but there was nothing I could do about them. The ground was frozen solid and the first flakes of a storm were falling. Burying all these aliens was out of the question. "If Earth's defenses shot them down, don't they know where they crashed?" I asked. "Where *you* crashed?"

"My ship is a stealth ship. It was under a distortion field. It was *cloaked,* as you would call it. Your authorities never knew I was there. But they will track the Shaax ship to where they believe it crashed. And they will find my ship, too."

"They won't be tracking anything in the storm we're about to get. I'll bring you back here after the blizzard ends. We'll deal with this, then."

I bit my lower lip. What was I thinking, bringing this alien male back to my home? My girls were there. But he'd saved my life from that alien dog. Virilians were *not* hostile.

And the truth was, if I called for help, my property would be swarmed with government people and, yes, that dog beast would be killed and maybe it shouldn't be. Any frightened creature would behave as it had, under bad circumstances.

And then there was Sakar. Earth had a zero-tolerance policy with uninvited aliens—prince or not. It was one thing every single country in the world agreed on. If the authorities took him, I could only imagine what his fate would be.

Sakar was not steady on his feet. I wrapped my arm tightly around his torso. We crossed the uneven clearing and returned to the UTV. I helped him into the seat beside mine. He filled up the entire front of the cab. His head barely cleared the metal bars above him. I started up the engine and was soothed by the familiar rumble of it.

I glanced over at the pale, exhausted alien beside me. This was my last chance to kick him out now. He was weak and I wouldn't get another opportunity to have the physical upper hand with him. But I had no reason to leave him here. He was here by accident. This was a risk my gut told me to take. I put the UTV into gear and drove us home.

CHAPTER 4

Sakar

I remembered a little of my journey in Nessa's vehicle. I had never been to Earth, but I had some general knowledge of the planet's environment, which was vastly varied. It had everything—deserts, ice caps, tropics, and this, a temperate forest region.

The trees here were tall and thick. Some were bare branches while others were covered in thin green needles. I held onto the metal frame that covered the seating area of this strange, small vehicle. With every bounce, my head pounded. I shut my eyes and gritted my teeth against the pain.

The female, Nessa, poked my arm. "Hang in there," she said. "Don't pass out until I get you home."

I had no intention of passing out, but rest sounded wonderful.

It occurred to me that I probably should've asked more questions. This female could have been taking me anywhere, but she had a matter-of-fact sense about her and I was in no position to argue. I also had no options. My head throbbed as if my skull was cracked. My vision was a mess. I *was* seeing double. It had been very disorienting when trying to soothe the *daerli*. And if a severe storm was to hit this area eminently, my disabled ship would not be a safe place to stay.

I blinked my eyes and looked up to see small white flakes coming through the branches overhead. The snow was falling faster and thicker now. Nessa's jaw was set in determination. She was probably second-guessing her decision to bring me back to her house and I could not blame her. After what she'd just witnessed, I was not sure I would pile an injured alien into my vehicle and bring him home either.

The forest ended in a clearing. I saw three structures ahead. The smallest was white with a pitched roof. Smoke puffed from a chimney and lights shone through the windows. This was probably Nessa's home. Something about it made me feel warm inside. There was a welcoming sense to this structure that made me yearn for something.

The two other structures were large and weather-beaten with giant rolling doors. One was white and the other red, although the paint appeared to be peeling off both. Nessa steered the vehicle to one of the large buildings. She hopped out, pushed open one of the doors, then returned and drove the vehicle inside. It was darker, but several large windows on the other side let in light.

"What is this?" I asked, looking around. It smelled strange in here.

"It's a barn," she replied. "There are some animals in here, as well as some equipment." She nodded toward several size-able life forms gazing at me from stalls. I hid my surprise at the sight of them. "They're not anywhere near the last of their species, but be respectful to them anyway," she said.

I eased myself off the small vehicle and approached one of them. "You keep these creatures contained in these small spaces?" The large brown creature gazed at me with soft eyes. It was chewing something.

"That's Peaches. She's a cow," Nessa replied. "And they're only in here during the day when the weather's bad and they can't get outside."

A cow. *Fascinating.* I knew the word, but now I knew what the animal looked like...and smelled like. "Peaches," I said, and the large creature mooed at me. "What about that one?" I pointed to the second cow, whose enormous hindquarters faced me.

"That's Harriet," she said. "You know my language, but—wait. *How* do you know it? Do you have one of those implant chips?"

I nodded. "I inserted it when I realized I was heading toward your planet."

She winced. "Does that hurt?"

"No." I turned my attention to the cow. "But it is an unnatural way to know another language. I know the words for things, but not what they *are.*"

She pulled a tarp over the vehicle we rode here in. "How do you mean?"

"I know a cow is a quadrupedal livestock animal that produces milk, meat and a few other products," I said. "But the language chip does not give me images or sensations to go with the words." I looked at her, or rather, *both* of her, since my double vision hadn't yet subsided completely. "Are they dangerous?"

"Depends," she replied with a chuckle. "Peaches doesn't bite, but her gas is lethal." She pointed across the barn to where another, different, four-legged animal stood in a different pen. "Prince Charming, on the other hand, *does* bite, so stay away from him. He's a horse, by the way."

"Oh, a horse. Primarily used for riding."

Nessa laughed. "Nobody dares ride him anymore. He's *not*

very charming. He'd toss anyone right off—even me. The chickens, over there," she nodded to where a cluster of fluffy beige birds sat on roosts, cooing quietly, "you should leave them alone, too. They peck."

I looked around at the creatures in this place and shook my head, which hurt. "Why do you have these animals?"

Nessa cut open a rectangular block of some tan straw in an unoccupied stall and proceeded to spread it out. "Because they live here. I'm not a farmer like my father was. I'm just way too soft for that, so they stay. They're like pets." She placed a stack of blankets on the straw and gestured for me to come to the stall. "You can rest here until I decide whether to let you in the house. Here are some blankets. The hay is warm and the animals keep the barn a decent temperature." Her eyes softened with apology. "I'm sorry. I have two children and I don't know you," she said, rubbing a hand over her forehead. "I just need to think, but if you need me, just come to the house."

I inclined my aching head. "I am grateful for a place to rest," I said. "And I am in your debt for not sending me off to your authorities. It would be a death sentence for the *daerli*, who I must locate as soon as possible."

"You're not going anywhere for a couple of days," she said, then winced. "If your *daerli* has any sense of self-preservation, it will find a sheltered spot and hunker down until this storm passes."

"They can endure harsh climates," I said. "He will survive whatever challenge your environment presents."

"We'll see." Nessa moved to the door. She had a graceful way of moving, all competence and strength. "I'll be back in a little bit with some food," she said. "Virilians eat human food, right?"

"I believe our diets are not so varied."

She nodded. "I've got soup on the stove. I'll bring you some clothing. Are you sure you're not freezing?"

"My kind are quite hot-blooded." She had no idea how much. Lying under the form I currently presented was a fiery hot being with flaming horns that could incinerate this barn. Fortunately, my primal form had not ever emerged. Nor was it likely to, ever. "Humans are more affected by temperature than us, it would seem."

She crossed her arms and studied me with a complicated expression. "So it would seem. It looks like you're going to be here for Christmas. That's not going to be awkward at all."

Christmas… The word was very uniquely human—another one that had a definition but no true meaning. "A winter holiday celebrated by some of your people."

"That's the one," she said. "The storm is supposed to park here until the day after."

I *was* glad for a place to rest. Outside I could hear the wind picking up and rattling the barn windows. Peaches let out a soft moo. Her companion remained in the corner munching on the same substance Nessa had provided for my bed. "I have no wish to disrupt your celebration."

She chuckled, a warm, throaty sound that hit me some-where low in the gut, pleasantly. "Too late. But it's no big deal —just the three of us. My two daughters and me. It's not much of a celebration. They usually play video games and I read a book. We eat a lot of food." She smiled sadly. "No other family left to celebrate with."

The way she said that made it clear how sad that made her. I inclined my head and sat on the bed of straw she had set out for me. "Nevertheless, I don't wish to be a bother. Pretend like I'm not here."

She shook her head, a tired smile curving her lips. "Yeah, right. You just upended my world, you know, by crashing into my forest, Sakar."

"I apologize for the damage to your trees." I gazed up into her eyes. I wished I could see the color in this dim light. Her face was…pretty, I thought distantly. She smelled like the trees and something bright, sweet. Most of her was bundled under her heavy layers of clothing, including her hair, but I knew the rest would be appealing. Maybe it was her voice, or the smooth way she moved, but I found myself interested in pleasing her. "But if I had to crash-land anywhere, I'm glad I did so here. You are compassionate and intelligent, Nessa." I raised one eyebrow. "Some would have shot me on sight."

"Humans are not that bloodthirsty," she said quietly. "Some of us are too soft for our own good." She put her hand on the door. "Get some rest, Sakar." She slid the door open enough to slip through, then disappeared into the swirling wind and snow. She closed the door quickly, sealing the storm out and throwing the barn into a peaceful quiet.

I spread a blanket over the straw—or hay, as she called it —and lay down, pulling another blanket over me. Virilians truly weren't as affected by the cold as humans were. Nessa had shivered, even with her thick garments. I was perfectly comfortable with the blanket and nothing else. Prince Charming, the horse, let out a snicker and stamped a hoof to the floor. The cows chewed their food. And in the far corner I heard the quiet trill of those plump birds—the chickens—as they found spots on their roosts to sleep. I closed my eyes and settled into the soft bed, letting the odd, strangely soothing sounds and smells of the barn work through me. I was so tired. The pounding in my head gave way to sleep. Soon, everything went soft and dark.

CHAPTER 5

Sakar

I didn't know how much time passed before I awoke, but a new sound pulled me from sleep. It was gentle snickering, whispers. I opened my eyes. The windows let in pale gray light. Wind and snow still pounded the barn. Movement directly above me caught my attention. In the rafters above me, two inquisitive faces peered down.

They were young human females. I laced my fingers behind my head as I regarded them. There was no question they were sisters. They had the same arch to their brows, which was identical to Nessa's. "Hello there."

They let out a peal of giggles. "Hi," said the younger one. Red-gold hair, barely contained in a braid, hung down beside her face. She looked at the girl beside her. "I told you he talked."

"I never said he didn't," replied the older one with a scowl. "I didn't think he spoke our language."

"Mom said he did."

"*Fine*. Quit it, Mia." The older girl, with a serious expression and hair tucked under a hat, was clearly vexed by the younger. "I didn't think he would talk to *us*."

"Why not?" the younger—Mia—said with a wide grin, thoroughly enjoying the act of annoying her sister. "We're nice humans."

"You must be Nessa's children," I said, stating the obvious, but eager to hold off a war between the two as they hung suspended above me. "I am Sakar. It is nice to meet you."

Their attention swung back to me. "I'm Violet and this is my sister, Mia. She's eight," the older one said in a disgusted tone, as if her sister's age was a burden to bear.

"How old are *you?*" asked Mia.

An interesting opening question. "Much older than you." I didn't know the equivalent in human years.

She rolled her eyes. "I knew *that*. You're like, older than my mom."

"Oh my god, Mia, that's rude," the older girl, Violet, hissed at her.

I chuckled. "It's quite all right."

"Do you have kids?" Mia went on, ignoring her sister's scowl.

"Sadly, no," I replied.

"I like your bracelets," said Mia. "Do they mean anything?"

All but one were mementos from past battles, but I wouldn't delve into that with these young ones. "The thick metal one, here," I pointed to the wide, metal band around my wrist, "is an emergency link with my ship."

"Cool." Violet squinted to get a better look. "Like, you can talk to it?"

"No. A button on it can make my ship take off and return to my home planet, in case of an emergency," I explained. "But I cannot leave until I find the creature I came to retrieve."

"Are you really a prince?" Both of their gazes pinned to me. This, clearly, was an important question.

I answered with the utmost gravity. "My cousin is a king, so yes. I am a prince."

"Wow," Mia breathed. "A real prince." Then, "Mom doesn't know we're here."

"I do not plan to tell her," I said with a wink. "Tell me, do you know how long I slept?"

"Since yesterday afternoon," said Violet. "So, like, twenty-four hours. A whole day."

Mia's mouth rounded. "Ooo, that's a long time. You must have to use the bathroom real bad."

I resisted the smile that pulled at my lips. "Where is your mother?" I asked. "I would very much like to speak with her."

"She's—" Mia began. The barn door slid open, emitting a gust of cold, snowy wind. "Uh-oh."

"Yes," said a stern voice. "Uh-oh." Nessa walked over and glared up at her daughters. "I told you specifically to not come in here and bother him."

"We were curious," said Violet. "We're sorry."

"Yeah," Mia piped up. "We *had* to see the alien man. He really is a prince! Is he staying for Christmas?"

That only made Nessa's scowl deepen. "Get down from there, both of you."

"They were no bother," I said, sitting up. "Children are curious. In Virilian, we have a word—*parokka*—which translates to *inquisitive young*. It's a state they are incapable of avoiding."

Nessa's mouth eased its tense line. "I should have threatened to take away their screens." She held a fabric pile and a metal cylinder. She placed the fabric on the ground near me. "Here are some clothes. The shirt was…well, it's been packed away in the attic for years, so apologies for the musty smell. It was all I had that might possibly fit you."

"Thank you." I watched the children scurry along the rafters, walking easily on planks placed on the beams above, then hop down a ladder. I smiled. "Your daughters are charming."

"Hmm." Nessa arched one eyebrow and raised her voice. "Since they're here, they can clean the cow and chicken pens."

Grumbling ensued, but both girls picked up shovels with ease and entered the cow area. They were greeted with moos from the large creatures.

Nessa handed me the cylinder and a utensil. "I came earlier with a thermos of soup, but you were still asleep. I hope you like chicken and dumplings."

I looked over to the pen where the chickens were pecking at the floor.

"Not them," said Nessa quickly. "They lay eggs and do their thing."

"Soup would be wonderful," I said, feeling the rumble in my stomach. I didn't care if the chickens were from here. There was no shame in raising livestock for food. I had a feeling that slaughtering animals was not something Nessa wanted any part in, though. She had a gentle heart. "Thank you."

She nodded and watched as I opened the container and breathed in the scent of the soup. It was so appealing, I almost shuddered, but it was the female in front of me that enticed me more. Without the double vision, I saw her features more clearly. She had high cheekbones, flushed from the cold, and warm eyes—not green, not brown, but a shade in between.

"How are you feeling today?" she asked, frowning at my forehead. "That's quite the bruise on your head."

I barely felt it. I dipped the spoon in the container and ate. "I feel much better," I replied. "And this is delicious."

She smiled. "Good. I'm going to help the girls get the

stalls cleaned out and the animals fed while there's a bit of a lull in the storm."

This was a lull? The wind battered relentlessly, slipping through cracks and rattling the windows. I rose, uncomfortable with sitting idly while three females worked around me, but Nessa held up a hand. "Stay there. Finish your soup."

Mia looked over longingly. "Why can't he help if he wants to?"

"Because he's never cleaned out animal pens before." She turned a raised brow to me. "Have you?"

"No," I confessed.

She nodded. "That's what I thought."

I watched as the three of them moved like a team. Nessa had the horse's pen cleaned out in no time. The girls petted and cooed over the cows, who butted them for more scratches on their cheeks. Violet collected eggs from the chickens' nesting boxes and spread fresh hay in their enclosure. None of them seemed to mind tending the animals. In fact, they treated them like adored pets, although no one smiled as they piled dung-filled straw into a cart.

"The animals like it better outside," Mia said to me as she put away her shovel. "So do I. They poop *so* much."

I laughed, deciding that I liked this child.

By the time they were done, the barn smelled considerably better. Feed had been dispensed. The animals were making approving chewing noises. The storm made it hard to do much out there, but the "poop cart," as Mia called it, had been emptied outside.

Nessa gazed at the barn door. "Guess we should shovel our way back to the house. It's only a few yards."

"It'll be back just as high five minutes later," Violet muttered. The girls seemed in no hurry to go back to their house. They sat on hay cubes, trying not to make it obvious that they were studying me.

"We shouldn't leave him in the barn," said Mia. "It's Christmas Eve. He should come to the house."

Nessa bit her lower lip and looked at me. "Virilians have been very good to humans," she said. "I have no reason to be afraid of you. You did save me from your *daerli*."

"I have no reason to harm you, either," I said. "But I can stay here if you would like." I said this, but I wanted to go in with them. In the short time I'd been with these three females, they'd enchanted me. The children were lively and charming, even the reserved and serious Violet.

And Nessa…she was intriguing on a different level. My gaze followed her wherever she moved. I found myself studying the sweep of bronze hair that escaped her hat and the light spray of freckles over her cheeks. She stuck her tongue out of one side of her mouth when lifting something heavy. She smiled quickly and easily when her daughters said something funny, which was often.

"Where is your mate?" I asked. It was a bit abrupt. No, it was *very* abrupt.

Nessa turned to me with surprise in her eyes. "My—my *mate?*" She blinked as if she'd run out of words. "Umm."

Violet pursed her lips. "Do you mean our dad? He died six years ago. We had a stepdad for a while. *Gavin.*" Her face screwed up into an angry scowl. "But he left."

"Left?" This concept confounded me. Who could possibly leave these females? "He was called away on an important duty?"

"No." Violet's shoulders jerked up to her ears as she frowned. "He left our mom for Tiffany, the lady who manages the Feeds and Needs farm store."

Nessa shot Violet a wide-eyed look. "Gavin and I weren't a good fit, obviously. Thank you, Violet, for that blunt summation."

Violet shrugged. "It's better without him here. We didn't

need him." Then under her breath, she muttered, "We don't need anyone."

Color had darkened Nessa's cheeks. "Well, that was more than you needed to know about the sad state of our family."

"There is nothing sad about this family," I said. "Anyone who would willingly leave you is obviously not worthy of you. *Any* of you," I added.

The three of them stared at me as if I had spoken in Virilian, but it was the truth. I inclined my head. "I am very sorry to hear about your first mate," I said. "Loss is never easy."

Nessa didn't say anything right away. She leaned her hip against the side of the stall and appeared deep in thought for a moment. Then, she lifted her head and looked at me, having clearly come to a decision. "Okay. You can stay in the house." She toed the neat pile of clothes on the floor before me. "But put a shirt on."

CHAPTER 6

Nessa

I didn't know what to expect.

It had been quite some time since a man had been in my home. Gavin didn't get visiting rights, since he wasn't the girls' father—although he had actually *tried* to get some custody during the divorce, just to needle me. And I had never, ever, had a male like *this* in my home.

Sakar filled the kitchen with more than his impressive size. He exuded power and primal strength, and that made it seem like he took up more space than he did. He looked around, taking in the strings of lights we had hung around the entryway from the kitchen to the living room, the stack of mail on the kitchen table, and the row of mugs that hung on pegs next to the unused phone jack.

The kitchen and dining area had, in my opinion, normal clutter. The fridge was covered in magnets, school schedules and cute notes the kids had made me. There was a picture of the four of us—the girls and me with Owen, before he passed, and on the counter were two pies that would remain untouched until the next day. Sakar raised his nose and sniffed. "I smell that soup," he said, like a wolf on the hunt.

"You can have more if you want," I told him. "I made a load of it."

He looked at me with hope shining in his eyes. "Really? I would love some more."

"Let's show you the rest of the house first," said Mia. She took his hand and pulled him toward the living room.

It was odd to see and a little jarring. Mia had typical, eight-year-old sized hands, but they looked like an infant's in comparison to Sakar's, whose hand engulfed hers. But he allowed her to pull him effortlessly into the next room. I followed, bemused. Violet gave them an uncertain look and followed in last.

There, I tried to see the scene as he would see it. Holiday music was playing, and would play continuously, through the next day. Our Christmas tree, a straggly balsam fir that we cut down from the woods a week ago was laden with ornaments, garland, and lights. It was holding up pretty well, valiantly trying to not sag under the weight of all of its decorations. Beneath the tree were some presents from the girls to each other and to me. The rest of their gifts would "appear" the next morning. The room smelled like pine and the cinnamon-vanilla candle winking away on the coffee table.

Sakar rubbed the tip of a branch between his fingers. "A tree in the house."

I crossed my arms. "It's a Christmas tree," I said. "It's not here all year round. Just for this holiday season."

"What a shame," he said, taking in the tree and its lights with an open face of wonder. It made his already handsome face breathtaking. "It's a lovely, interesting thing."

He was a lot to have in my house. Seeing him there, standing beside my daughter, brought up feelings I had thought long extinguished. I took in the breadth of his shoulders, straining against the flannel shirt I'd given him and the shape of his ass in those tight pants. My imagination spiraled off, wondering what it would feel like to have his arms around me. What his mouth would feel like on mine. I imagined exploring that rigid stretch of muscled abdomen, testing the weight of that huge bulge below. My mouth went dry and my breasts tingled. Desire surprised me with dampness between my legs as my thoughts turned carnal.

Then, as if he could sense my arousal, his gaze snapped to mine, hot and sharp and aware. His nostrils flared and his head came up just a little, as if smelling something in the air other than the cinnamon-vanilla candle and the Christmas tree.

Could he...*smell me?* That bulge in his pants didn't leave much to the imagination, but it also didn't have much room for expansion, if I did inspire a similar degree of attraction in him. It wasn't likely. A divorced mom in her forties wasn't going to catch the eye of a male like this. Sakar made the hottest Hollywood actor look dumpy.

"Mom, somebody called your phone while we were out." Violet pointed to my phone, which sat face up on the kitchen table. I opened it to see an unknown number. They had left a message. I listened to it, and my gut dropped.

Good afternoon, Ms. Thompson, this is the Department of Planetary Security. There have been reports of some unusual spacecraft activity in your area. If you have seen or heard of anything questionable, please call us at... They left a number and then hung up, but I had a feeling they would call again. I looked through the archway into the living room where Mia was pointing out her favorite ornaments to the *very* illegal alien standing beside her.

Violet looked at me from the corners of her eyes. "Are we going to get in trouble for keeping him here?"

"Absolutely not." I crossed my arms. "He's not a criminal. Just the opposite. He saved my life out there. I owe him a lot more than a hot meal and a place to sleep."

Violet looked up at me confused. "Why are the governments of Earth so worried about them?"

My mouth compressed, ready to give her an answer neither of us would like. "Because Virilians are strong and advanced enough to take over our planet if they want to. That's what scares our governments. That's why they restrict them from coming here."

"But if they could take over our planet, what's the point of all of these restrictions? I mean, they must just find them funny."

"They kind of *are* funny if you look at it like that," I said to her. "And more importantly, they haven't tried to take us over. They have their own planet and in return for, well, dating human women, they consider us under their protection."

I knew she wanted to ask more questions. She knew darn well all about the Virilian match program, but not the nitty-gritty details. Not the part about producing children for them. She was only eleven. We could get into that a little later on. It just made everything more complicated between our two people. There was absolutely no doubt in my mind that ego played some role in all of this. Human women found Virilians very exciting and attractive. Little wonder our men didn't want Virilians showing up here en masse.

But I had one right here in my living room, smiling and even chuckling over something my youngest daughter was saying. He wore my late husband's flannel lumberjack shirt. It was tight, stretching over his wide pectoral muscles. His biceps bulged out the sleeves. He still wore those tight leather pants that allowed his tail to come out. He kept it carefully away from Mia, mindful of the wicked barb on the end of it.

Yes, I *definitely* saw what human men were worried about. Add that to the fact that the Virilians were known for treating their mates like queens and I could see why there were so many rules about them coming here. I glanced back to my phone on the table. The storm was keeping anyone from coming here, for now, but it would not remain that way. As soon as the roads became passable and the snow stopped, these woods would have government officials in them. They knew generally where that ship went down. They didn't know who was in it.

I chewed on my bottom lip as I thought about options. If we could get Sakar's ship out of the woods, they would only find the other crashed one—what had Sakar called them? I couldn't remember. Something that started with an S.

"What shape is the guest room in?" I asked Violet. She used that room to read in because she liked the big armchair I kept in there.

"It's good," she said. "Is that where he's going to stay?"

"I'm not going to kick him back into the barn, if that's what you're asking."

"How long is he staying?" Violet asked.

"Until he can get to his ship and fly out of here," I replied with a weird lump in my throat. "As soon as possible."

She gave me a hard look. "You're not gonna do anything silly and fall in love with him, are you? 'Cause that didn't work out well last time."

It was my turn to give her a sharp look. "I'm not planning on doing anything of the sort," I said. "And give me a break about Gavin, will you? Wait till you're older. See if you make all the right choices in relationships." The truth was, I felt really bad about how things went with my ex. The girls had gotten attached to Gavin. I thought he was a good, steady guy and would be a father to them. He didn't try to take their real father's place. He didn't try to come between us, and he certainly didn't try to hoard my attention. It had seemed like a good situation. And we got along. I thought maybe I loved him, or could learn to. Looking back, my first mistake had been right there.

Mia pointed way high up in the tree to something she couldn't reach. Sakar stooped down and lifted her effortlessly up, using his forearm as a seat for her. I'd never seen anyone be picked up like that. He must have enormous strength. Mia plucked the ornament she wanted to show him off the tree. It was a tiny wind-up music box that began to play Jingle Bells in a discordant tune that clashed with the music coming through the speakers. But she laughed anyway before replacing it on the tree. With utmost care, Sakar placed her back down.

Violet watched all this. I could see on her face she didn't know what to make of him. We could agree on that. I had no clue what to think of our visitor.

"Who wants soup?" I asked. Sakar and Mia turned around simultaneously.

"Me!" my daughter called. "I'm hungry."

Sakar smiled, wide and full and gut-punchingly gorgeous. "I would like more soup, Nessa."

Good grief, even the way he said my name made my knees weak. "Okay," I said a little breathlessly. "Let's go. Violet, can you set the table please?"

She sighed and did as I asked. I set out the pot of soup and a hunk of sourdough bread I'd made that morning.

I thought the four of us sitting down to eat would be awkward, but it wasn't. We were all hungry and dug in quickly. The girls and I sat in our usual seats, and Sakar took the empty one, where every man who'd ever lived in this house had sat. He looked both natural and alien sitting there.

The dark skin around his eyes crinkled as he smiled at whatever outlandishly enhanced "true" story Mia told him. His fangs flashed, reminding all of us that he was different and by far the most powerful creature to ever step foot in this old farmhouse.

I could see that he was trying to restrain himself from eating too much, so after his first bowl, I just scooped more in.

He looked at me gratefully. "We Virilians heal quickly, but it requires a lot of fuel to do so."

"Well then, eat as much as you want," I said. "We're going to need to get your ship out of my woods as soon as the storm ends."

His eyes sharpened. "Have you heard something?"

I shrugged. "I got a call. They know something happened around here, but not what. We have time. The storm isn't going anywhere until the day after tomorrow."

Mia's brow furrowed. "Is Sakar in trouble?"

"No, sweetie. No one's in trouble."

Violet kept quiet. She was a little more savvy and pragmatic than Mia.

Sakar walked to me. His steps were deliberate. He held my gaze and stopped right before me, a hairsbreadth away. I could feel the warmth of his body coming off of him, teasing with my own. "I will not allow harm to come to your family," he said. "I will walk out in the storm if need be."

Something in my chest tightened and unfurled at the same time. My mouth went dry. I wasn't even sure how to respond. It was the most thoughtful thing anyone had said to me in a long time. "That won't be necessary," I said. "You'll stay for Christmas. And you're not going out in the storm. I don't want harm to come to you, either. Not after you saved my life from that…"

"Daerli," he supplied. "And I must find him, as well, before I leave."

"Do you think he's strong enough to survive the storm?"

"Yes," Sakar replied. "He would curl up and sleep under all the snow. But when it ends, he will be hungry. Do the other humans around here have animals they keep, like you do?"

"Yes, they have animals, but they keep them like normal farmers. As in, not pets."

"Then those animals are in danger," he said. "And potentially so are their owners." He frowned. "I am sorry this trouble came to you. I will do everything I can to—"

"I know you will," I said, cutting him off. "For now, there's a storm outside and a holiday to celebrate."

He smiled, making my stupid knees feel weak again. His fingers brushed my forearm so gently, my heart stammered. "Thank you, Nessa. It would be an honor."

I stepped back, resisting the urge to rub my arm where he had touched me, where a riot of sensations spiraled over my skin. "Okay." I looked at the girls, who had watched this scene like it was their favorite YouTube show. Violet wore a little frown. "Who wants hot chocolate?" I asked them.

Mia's arm shot into the air. "Me!"

"I'll take some," said Violet. "With a candy cane, please."

I raised an eyebrow toward Sakar. "It's a sweet drink. Want to try it?"

"Is it a Christmas tradition?"

"For us, it absolutely is," I replied. "Along with cookies and a civil, no-yelling board game."

"It's *not* friendly," said Violet. "Mia cheats."

Mia's face turned red with fury. "I do not!"

I shook my head and went to the kitchen while the two of them worked it out. Sakar followed. "Siblings," I said with an eye roll. "Do you have one?"

"A brother or sister? No. But I have a younger cousin who is like a brother to me."

"Oh? Nice. I don't have any siblings or cousins that I'm close to," I said. "What is your job on Virilia, aside from chasing down endangered species?"

"I am a high advisor to King Virak of Tagja City." He picked up a salt shaker in the shape of a fat white cat. "And his chief commander."

I almost dropped the mug I was holding. "That sounds like an important job."

"It is. I led the resistance against raiders who sought to control Virilia. The Sifters were uniquely challenging and they were led by a power-hungry leader. Now that they are defeated, I have assumed the role of my cousin's advisor and I do missions, like this."

Even I knew who King Virak was. He had been matched with a human woman who was now their queen. It certainly made the relationship between humans and Virilians a little more complex.

"Wait a minute," I said, realizing I had overlooked a key detail here. "Are you saying your cousin is King Virak?"

He nodded, as if this was no big deal. "He is a good king. Fair. Reserved. And he has a passion for rescuing creatures that are rare and trafficked." He held up the salt shaker. "What is this for?"

I took it out of his hand and shook a bit of salt into his palm. "It's for salting food. Give it a little taste."

He held my gaze as he lifted his hand to his mouth. His tongue came out and touched the salt, then drew it back into his mouth. He smiled. "We have this on our planet, too."

I picked up the matching shaker. It looked like the other, except it was a black cat. "This one is for pepper. It tastes very different."

He wanted to taste that one, too, so I did the same and

shook a tiny bit into his hand. "Just a little," I said. "It's, well, peppery."

He didn't really listen and licked all of it up on his tongue.

I couldn't help but laugh as his features pinched and he shook his head like a dog who had just been stung on the nose by a bee. "I told you."

"That is not a pleasant taste."

"Not alone, like that," I said, taking the shakers and putting them on the counter. "They're used to season food. Believe it or not, it's in that soup you like so much."

He looked skeptical at that. "I do not like it," he declared.

I laughed again, feeling more and more at ease with him. "That's okay. There's none of it in hot chocolate, so you don't need to worry."

He watched as I prepared the hot cocoa. I wished I could say I made it from scratch, but I opened four packets of Swiss Miss and dumped each in a mug. I added hot milk, stirred, and dropped a candy cane in each. I handed him one.

He took a cautious sip, then his eyes closed and his lips curved into a blissful smile. "This, on the other hand, is delicious."

I took a sip of my own. "I'm glad you like it."

His gaze moved over my face. Then dropped to my mouth. "It is not all I like."

I did *not* choke on my cocoa. I managed to spit it back in my mug before that happened. "What now?"

"Hmm. You have some cocoa on your upper lip." He reached out slowly, as if half expecting me to jerk away. But I was frozen in place, locked there by a pair of brilliant blue eyes and the impossible-to-ignore desire to be touched by him. His thumb traced over the line of my upper lip. My mouth opened on a gasp. My body swayed toward his, pulled forward with the need to be closer. His thumb lingered at the corner of my mouth. His fingers splayed over my cheek.

"Beautiful," he murmured.

Was he talking about me? I hadn't been called beautiful in a long time. Maybe that was partially my own doing. I was so busy, I didn't spend much time on myself. My hair was usually up in a sloppy bun or under a hat. I rarely wore makeup, and my clothes were of the practical type, which did not exactly flatter a figure. Though, I did so much physical work around here, that my figure was holding up pretty well. I was strong. It was impossible not to be when moving hay bales and hauling wood. I blinked up at him. I didn't know what to say. Maybe I'd misheard him.

"I did not enter myself into the Virilian match program," he said quietly. "But if I had, I would want to be matched with you."

Okay. There was no ambiguity there. No one else in the room to be mistaken for. Desire snaked through my body like electricity, waking up all the parts that had gone dormant.

I opened my mouth to reply with something—anything— but all that came out was a weird little croak that sounded a little bit like, "Oh?"

He lowered his gaze. "Both the timing and the circumstances are horrendous," he said. "But when I smelled your arousal, earlier, my own answered. I don't understand this, Nessa, but I am drawn to you."

He didn't understand it? The alien male had been in my house for a couple hours and he was telling me he wished we were matched. Not only that, I was standing there wishing the same exact thing.

My head swam. I couldn't look away from him. The hand on my face slid down my neck to my shoulder. He gently pulled me toward him, and I, completely at the whim of my desires, placed a hand on his wide, muscular chest.

His head lowered, his lips parted, and a voice from the

living room cut through this insanity. "Is the hot cocoa ready yet?"

I stepped back, dragging in a ragged breath. I couldn't look at him or I'd be right back in his arms. "Coming," I called back to Mia in a pitchy voice. With shaking hands, I turned away, blindly grabbed the girls' and my mugs, and brought them out to the living room.

CHAPTER 7

Sakar

I couldn't think. I could hardly breathe. I wasn't completely sure what had just happened. Longing, a level of which I had never known before, squeezed my chest, causing an ache I wasn't sure what to do with. My breathing was ragged and my head was a mess of thoughts, most of them so filthy I couldn't put them into words.

I knew I found Nessa attractive, but I was not expecting *this*. I didn't dare ponder what it meant. The words I had said to her had come as a surprise, even to me. Was it true? Was this female my match?

I picked up the cup of cocoa in my rubbery hands. I sipped it, letting that sweet taste roll over my tongue, knowing the taste of Nessa would be even more delicious.

I slowly made my way back to the living room. There, the three females were looking through a stack of colorful, rectangular boxes. Nessa looked up at me. I braced myself for anything from cold rejection to anger. But instead, what I saw was a soft shyness that took me by surprise.

She smiled and patted the couch cushion next to her. "We're picking out a game," she said. "Trying to find one that wouldn't be too hard for you to learn."

I crossed to them and sat beside her. Mia and Violet had narrowed the choice down to two. Finally, one game emerged as the winner. It was in a small, red box. Mia held it up triumphantly. "Uno." She sent an accusatory glance to her sister. "By the time we explain how to play Monopoly, it will be our bedtime."

Violet rolled her eyes. "But it's not a board game."

"We can play it on the Monopoly board," her sister rebutted. "Would that help?"

That ended the discussion and I learned the mechanics of playing Uno. I gamely lost multiple times until I figured out the patterns and strategies of the clever little card game. By our fifth game of it, the plate of cookies had been demolished, the cocoa mugs were empty, and we were all laughing. The lights flickered. Nessa sent a frown toward the nearest lamp. "I hope we don't lose power," she muttered.

"Why would you?" I asked.

"Storms like this can knock out power," she explained. "Sometimes, for days."

"Which is fine sometimes," added Violet, "but not in the middle of winter."

I glanced over at the wood-burning stove, which crackled and gave off plenty of heat. I was appalled at the thought that their society would allow the power to go down. How poor was their infrastructure? "At least you won't freeze with this device." I had thought that burning wood was primitive, perhaps just for the effects, but no, it was a practical heat source.

"No," she replied. "But the pipes could freeze if the power is off long enough—that's never happened, though." She held up her hands so the girls would not worry. "This house has stood here for one hundred and forty years without a pipe bursting. Now, as for you two…" She moved her finger between Violet and Mia. "It's time to brush your teeth and get to bed. Or *you-know-who* isn't coming tonight." Violet rolled her eyes again. It seemed to be one of her favorite expressions, but she got up, kissed her mother's cheek, and went upstairs with Mia.

Nessa let out a long sigh. Her body relaxed as she collected the cards and slid them neatly back into their box. She kept her gaze away from me, however.

I was not one to let things fester, though. My blunt nature simply didn't tolerate it. "Shall we discuss what happened in the kitchen?"

Her hands tightened on the box of cards. "I'm not sure what to say. It was… I don't know."

It was not a rejection, at least. It was more than I could've hoped for from a female I'd just met and who was apparently quite potent to my senses.

"Nessa, I have never behaved in such a way to a female before. I have encountered many in my travels, of many species, but lust has not overtaken me as it did today. I confess, I want you even now. It takes effort to not reach for you, to not touch you."

She shivered, as her body reacted to my words. "I don't know you," she said. "You're…" She rolled her hand as if searching for the right word. "You're an alien, and I didn't sign up for the Virilian match program. It's insane to even think about…"

I raked my hands through my hair. I knew better than to question these things, and the feelings uncoiling in my chest, sending out tendrils of awareness, were making me more and more sure that this female was important to me. Perhaps more important than I could comprehend right now.

"Do you know how the Virilian match program works?" I asked.

She shook her head. "They're secretive about the process."

"Our powerful sages—seers, those with special sight—speak with those who have applied to the program, then they come to Earth after taking in what they know of those males and they feel the energy of the females they encounter. The sages are blind. They cannot see with their eyes, but only with their spirits. When they choose the right match, it is a match of the heart. The couple does not need to know each other deeply to be connected. It is, as you say on Earth, love at first sight."

She raised one eyebrow. "Not all of those matches are forever matches. Some have a baby, collect their money, and return to Earth."

I inclined my head. "Yes. But it is still a successful match. Both parties get what they want out of the arrangement."

"I hadn't thought of that before," she said. "I had assumed that the matches that didn't stay together were failures."

"I don't believe they are," I replied. "Nor do the sages, or the people matched."

She looked at her lap as if she were contemplating all this. When she looked up at me, her eyes were misty. "It doesn't really matter though, does it?" There was an edge of bitterness to her voice. "I'm here and your life is up there." She pointed to the ceiling. "It can't possibly work with us, and this is way too sudden."

I took her hand. It was tough with calluses and fit in mine perfectly. "I know that too," I murmured. "Perhaps, we only have these few days. However much or little time we have together, I will cherish it." I hated the finality of my words. It made my growing feelings for her sound hopeless.

Her fingers curled around mine. The lights flickered again as the wind howled.

Then she pulled her hand away and stood up. "My Christmas Eve tradition at this point is to get a glass of wine and read a book. I'll skip the book, but if wine was ever appropriate, it is now. I'll pour you a glass, too."

She left for the kitchen, leaving me in her cheery, warm living room, and returned a few moments later with two glasses of red liquid. She handed one to me and took her spot again on the couch, this time with her knees pulled up and facing me.

I sipped. This was wildly different from the cocoa. It was tart and rich, and reminded me of some drinks on Virilia.

"Sakar, I don't know what's true right now. Maybe I'm suffering from a delusion, but you've already upended my life, and I won't pretend that I'm not attracted to you." She placed her wine glass on the dining room table and looked at me again. Her eyes were wide and soft. Her lips were soft, pink pillows that were slightly parted. "Kiss me, Sakar. I want to know."

I shifted toward her. My fingers grazed her knee, covered in red leggings with white snowflakes. "Know what?"

"What you feel like." Her pupils dilated. "What you taste like. Everything."

"Everything?" That was a big word with huge implications.

She reached out and placed a hand on my chest. "Just a kiss. That's all I want." Her eyes went dark. "For tonight."

I did not pounce on her, but the wild creature that paced its cage inside of me, wanted to. I eased toward her and pulled her toward me. My mouth found hers ready and eager. She moaned as my lips slanted against hers. Her lips parted and her tongue met mine in a dance, scattering my thoughts and making me pull her even closer. I ran my hands through her hair and down her arms. My fingers found her spine and traced the delicate line down to the curve of her bottom. It was as if I already knew the shape of her and was coming home to it after a long time. Any doubts that this female was mine scattered to the winds that roared outside.

Mine. The word wound through my head. I knew from this kiss that there would not be another female for me. That she was the one my heart recognized. The one my soul would always yearn for.

Nessa's hands were not idle. She slid them over my chest, down my arms, squeezing the muscles there, which was interesting, but whatever pleased her. Her fingers trailed over my abdomen and the muscles there tightened. My tail slid over her legs, between her thighs but not venturing higher. My cock strained against my pants, raging to be released and be allowed to fully claim my female. But Nessa wanted to kiss and that was what we would do for as long as she wished. I would not press for more. Any touch from her was a gift.

I closed my eyes and sank into the scent and feeling of her. Sensations rolled through my body like rapid-fire explosions. She let out a little moan and need opened inside of me like a bloom. I vaguely heard the sounds of cheerful music, the crackling fire, and the storm. Her hands threaded into my hair and I shuddered. I kept an iron grip on my control, when all I wanted to do was strip her naked and fill her with my cock.

The lights flickered again and it knocked her out of our sexual haze. She leaned back and blinked as if trying to orient herself. Then she pushed me back gently with her hand and shook her head. "Wow," she said. "Just…wow."

I nodded, working hard to reel myself in and collect my bearings. I felt like an animal was inside of me, roaring and scratching to be released. To claim his mate. *My* mate.

I had never known feelings like this before, but it was exactly the way discovering one's mate was described to me by my own father: *You will know when you have met her,* he had told me. *It will be a singular, undeniable feeling.*

I had that feeling, with this human, in this impossible situation.

"It's late," she said in a high, breathy voice. Color rode high on her cheeks. Her lips were full and flushed, and her eyes were heavy with arousal. The scent of her was over-whelming. I knew she was wet for me. That her body was ready. But she was not ready in her mind, which was as important as the body.

She finished off her glass of wine and took both of our glasses into the kitchen. When she returned, she looked more composed. "I have to get the kids' gifts," she said, looking a little awkward.

I rose. "Let me help."

She smiled. "That would be great, thanks."

I followed her through the house to a dim basement, where behind some boxes she had a plastic tub filled with brightly wrapped gifts. She placed it in my arms, then moved to my side and peered at me worriedly. "Is this too heavy?"

I chuckled softly. "No," I said gently. "I am fairly strong for one of my species."

Her gaze moved appreciatively over my body. I liked the feeling of her eyes on me. "I can see that," she said seductively.

I did *not* drop the tub and yank her into my arms again, although I wanted to. Instead, I followed her up the stairs and arranged the girls' gifts on either side of the tree, so there would be no question whose were whose—she explained that had been an issue in previous years.

It was quite late. Even I was feeling fatigued. My body was still healing.

"Come," she said, holding out her hand. "Let's go to bed."

It was music to my ears, but I knew it would not be her

bed we would be retiring to, and there would be no sex tonight. I wouldn't assume that there would ever be. Nessa had been through a lot in her life, and was raising two lovely children on her own. She deserved to be cautious in her choices, and a stranded alien was not exactly an ideal choice for a bedmate. I took her hand and went upstairs with her.

She stopped in front of a door and pushed it open. "This is the guest room," she said. "All yours."

"Thank you." I placed my hands on her waist and gently drew her toward me. She didn't resist. Her arms twined around my neck and she lifted her face to mine. I lowered my mouth to hers and kissed her sweetly—*far* more sweetly than I wished to, but this was a good-night kiss and nothing more. I broke it off and reluctantly released her. "Good night, sweet Nessa." I went into the room.

"Good night," she whispered. I caught one last look from wide, luminous eyes as she closed the door with a decisive click.

The room was dark. I saw the large bed and every ache and sore place in my body reminded me I needed rest. I settled into bed, and after my body calmed down from its vivid yearnings, I fell fast asleep.

CHAPTER 8

Nessa

I expected Christmas Day to be a nightmare of awkwardness for Sakar and me, but it turned out to be one of the best holidays I'd had since before Owen died. The wind outside was not as pounding as it had been the day before. This was good, but it also meant that Sakar's ship needed to be moved sooner rather than later. As soon as the storm ended, the Department of Planetary Security would be here to survey, scan, and check the area.

The girls, of course, were up early, as always. I managed to get downstairs, put on a pot of coffee, and stoke up the fire again from the coals that had burned low overnight before they ripped into their gifts.

To my surprise, Sakar was already up with them. He wore the same clothes as yesterday, minus his boots. I reminded myself to find him a new shirt sometime today. He sat in the armchair closest to the tree, looking barefoot and comfortable, as Mia shook gifts and tried to guess what was inside.

"Do you think there might be a hamster in one of these?" she asked. "Because I'm really hoping to get a hamster."

His brows went up. "I doubt there are any living creatures inside these packages," he said sagely. "Unless it is in a deep cryogenic sleep." He raised one dark eyebrow. "Do your people have the capabilities of putting living creatures into stasis and successfully reviving them?"

Mia looked at him like he had just said the funniest thing in the world. "Maybe," she replied with a giggle. "You're so funny, Sakar."

Violet shook her head. "Mia, Mom said no to a hamster after what happened to the last one."

Mia's bottom lip poked out. "That was an accident. We said we'd never speak of it again."

I would not be enlightening Sakar on the sad fate of Vanilla the hamster, who escaped her cage when we were cat-sitting Mary Donough's Maine coon, Ms. Fluffin. I shuffled out into the living room in my bathrobe, clutching a cup of coffee. "Here." I handed it to him. "Taste it. If you like it, it's yours. I'll fix another one."

He took the mug. His gaze lit up. A splash of half-and-half had turned the coffee caramel colored. "It looks like cocoa," he said hopefully.

"It's not cocoa," I said. "Tastes totally different, but it helps wake you up."

He took a sip, thought for a moment, then handed the mug back to me with a pinched expression. "Not for me. But, thank you."

I chuckled and took the mug back. "No problem." I settled down on the couch to watch my girls open presents. The next half hour was a flurry of wrapping paper, delighted giggles, and the occasional, *do we have any AAA batteries?* The answer was no.

I opened gifts that the girls had given me and they opened

their gifts from each other, and from their grandparents. Sakar was the only one who did not receive anything, until Mia pulled a small package out from behind the tree. "This is for you," she said. "We didn't have much time to make it, but everyone should open something on Christmas."

He accepted the small, badly wrapped gift as if she had just handed him a priceless jewel. He looked up at her with soft eyes. "Thank you, Mia."

"I helped, too," said Violet. She crossed her arms and tried her best to glare at him, but couldn't quite pull it off. Despite her preteen attitude, Violet liked him, just like we all did. Maybe she didn't *want* to like him, but that put her in the same boat as the rest of us—liking someone who was destined to leave.

Sakar held the gift as if he was just cherishing the moment and didn't want to open it. His gaze moved over the three of us with affection. Then, he carefully pried open the copious amounts of tape to reveal what was inside. I had no idea the girls were doing this and I was just as curious as he was. Mia leaned forward, bottom lip between her teeth and her eyes wide with anticipation. Even Violet had a smile on her face.

My breath caught when I saw what Sakar held in his hands. It was a white ceramic mug that had belonged to Owen, the girls' father. Inside it was a packet of Swiss Miss hot chocolate mix.

Originally, the words on the mug read, *I'm a doctor, not an escalator*, with an illustration of the Star Trek character Dr. McCoy on it. Owen had been a big fan of the old Star Trek series and most of the series that came after. But after daily use, the printed words had worn off a bit, and the girls had decided to customize it. It now read, *I'm a Virilian, not an alien.* The added words were printed precisely with a Sharpie marker.

I stared, frozen in place as I watched Sakar hold the mug. I thought about the man who had drank out of it every morning. I'd bought it for Owen the year we were engaged. The girls smiled and bounced a little, oblivious to the fact that they had just handed their father's favorite mug over to our alien guest.

Sakar smiled, wide and full. He was absurdly handsome, but this smile brought his looks to a new level. But then he looked up at me and the smile faded. He looked down at the mug and comprehension dawned on his face. He knew whose mug this had been.

He set it on the coffee table and gave Mia and Violet sad smiles. "Thank you both. You're very thoughtful, but I'm not sure this mug can belong to me."

The girls looked over at me with surprise in their eyes. To them, it was just an unused mug that was perfect for the alien guy staying at our house. They were kids being generous and a mug was a thing that should be used, not sit untouched in a cabinet. Here it was, bringing joy to Sakar and my girls, who were so pleased with their clever gift.

I pulled in a deep breath and smiled at the three of them. "Absolutely not," I said. "It's a thoughtful and very cool gift. And you spelled Virilian correctly, Vi. Well done."

They smiled and went back to their gifts. I got up and moved toward the kitchen and the back door, where duty called. "I'm going to go take care of the animals," I said. "I'll be back shortly."

Sakar rose as well. "I will help you."

I wasn't going to turn down help. I nodded and we both donned winter gear. I found an old coat that was probably my father's, wool gloves, and he pulled on his boots. We grabbed the snow shovels at the back door and went outside.

The snow was deep. I groaned because even though it was a short distance to the barn, it came up past my knees. I had a system for when it was this deep. Scoop the top half, then the bottom, because all of it was too heavy to lift when it drifted up like this. But Sakar shoveled it effortlessly and quickly, with smooth even strokes.

I stepped back and let him. In no time, he cleared the path to the barn. Inside, I turned on the lights and took in the smell of hay. We were greeted with the usual moos, clucks, and whinnies.

"How did your husband die?"

The question didn't bother me, but it was jarring. I could tell he'd been wondering about this for a while. "Two things," I replied. "He was in a car accident, but he had a heart condition that no one knew about. The accident caused a heart attack."

Sakar nodded, frowning. "I'm sorry. I will not take that mug. It clearly had meaning for you."

I touched his arm. "No. You *will* take it. They gave it to you and I want you to have it so you…remember us."

His hair was damp from melted snow. "I don't need a mug to remember you, Nessa. I will never forget you."

The yearning in his voice answered something in mine. When his hand wrapped around the back of my neck and pulled me toward him, I was open and ready. This kiss tasted hungry, aching, like a love story that we both knew would end tragically.

We came apart on hard gasps. His breathing was shallow and labored. The blue of his eyes was almost crystalline with intensity.

With trembling hands, I picked up the shovel and pitchfork I needed to clean out the cow stall and take care of the horse.

Sakar did the same, knowing what to do without me having to direct him. I assumed he had watched us work the day before. It wasn't difficult to tend to the animals. It was just a bit of hard work.

Together, we had the pens cleaned out, the animals fed and watered, and I carried a basket of eggs back to the house.

"The snow is not falling as hard," he observed.

"I know," I said. "Tonight we should return to the crash site and get your ship back here…assuming it will fly. Tomorrow there will be government officials looking in the woods."

His nostrils flared. "Tonight then," he said. "After the girls are in bed."

We didn't speak about it for the rest of the day. We ate a huge meal of ham, mashed potatoes, and green beans, followed by homemade eggnog and the pies I had made the day before. The girls stayed in their pajamas all day. They settled in for some video game time, followed by digging into the new books they received for Christmas.

It was, by far, one of the more delightful holidays we'd had in a long, long time. My ex-husband had never made holidays fun. They were serious business. We spent them with his family, who were serious and formal. His mother had an enormous number of rules, which the girls struggled to remember. I could see why they didn't miss him. I didn't, either. But I would miss Sakar when he left.

That evening, Mia fell asleep in front of the wood stove. Violet didn't want to go to bed because she was enjoying her new book. Sakar carefully, with the utmost gentleness, picked up my youngest daughter and cradled her in his arms. The soft look on his face made my heart squeeze. I nodded toward the stairs and gave Violet a smile. "Come on up, sweetie," I said. "You can keep reading in bed."

Violet pried herself out of the chair and followed us up. It felt oddly like a regular family. Sakar fit in so well. Mia snuggled against him, murmuring in her sleep. I sent Violet to brush her teeth and helped him tuck Mia in. He laid her on the mattress. I tucked the comforter around her. Back out in the hallway, Violet was leaving the bathroom. She looked up at Sakar with wide eyes. "Thanks," she said.

"For what?" he asked.

"For being nice to us," she said. "My mom likes you. I'm sorry you have to leave." Then she did something utterly unexpected. She came forward and hugged him. Sakar's arms slowly closed around her. Violet squeezed her eyes shut, then stepped away and slipped into her room. The door closed.

I blinked away tears. "Wow. That was very un-Violet-like."

Sakar pulled in a shaky breath. "Your children are amazing." He turned his gaze to me. "You are... *Stars*. How can I leave you, Nessa?"

My tears weren't going away. "You have to. The government won't let you stay. They have strong rules about that."

"What if you—?"

"Why don't we go get your ship?" I said quickly to cut him off. I knew what he was going to say. He was going to ask us to go with him, but that sounded more impossible than him staying here. I had a job—a couple jobs—and girls to raise. They had school and I had the animals to care for. If I disappeared, what would happen to my parents' farm? True, it wasn't being used as a farm anymore, but I loved it here. I didn't want to abandon it.

He nodded. "Of course. Let's go to the ship."

It was smart to go now, before the snow stopped completely. We wouldn't be able to take the UTV. We'd have to take the snowmobile, but I feared even if it continued to snow, tracks would be visible to the authorities when they arrived. That was just a chance we'd have to take.

The snowmobile was a much snugger fit for the two of us. Sakar's thighs braced on either side of my hips. His chest was a solid, warm wall at my back. I shivered, aware of every inch of his body so close to mine. I shoved away the thoughts and concentrated on getting us where we needed to go. The vehicle was designed to drive through snow, but it was going to be rough going with snow this deep.

Still, this particular toy of Gavin's, which he'd forgotten to take when he left, came in handy. I started up the snow-mobile and took us down the wide path, then through the woods to the crash site. After all the snow, the area looked like boulders covered in snow drifts. At first glance, one wouldn't know that two spacecrafts and the bodies of dead aliens lay under all that white stuff.

I turned off the snowmobile. We got off and walked up to the stretch of flattened trees.

"Amazing that you found this place," Sakar said in awe. "The forest looked the same to me."

"I know these woods well," I said. "I've lived here for most of my life."

He pointed to a large mound ahead of us. "Let's see if my ship can get off the ground."

He cleared the snow from the large hatch and pressed his hand to a panel beside it. It opened and he stepped inside. "Come on. Let me show you my ship."

I hesitated, but then I followed, curious beyond words. I'd never seen the inside of an alien spacecraft before. I was not disappointed. The interior was unique and sleek, with dull metal walls and gleaming glass windows. As we went through, Sakar stopped at various panels with screens. He tapped them and they woke up one by one. Dim interior lights illuminated the cabin and passageways.

"I can make it brighter, if you like," he said. "It's set for Virilian eyes, which see better in lower light than human eyes."

"The lighting is fine," I said, looking around, gaping. "This is incredible. I wish the girls could see this," I said, and then wished I could take it back.

His gaze flicked to mine. "They can. You can come with me, Nessa. All three of you would be welcome on Virilia."

I ran a finger over the smooth line of a chair in the main cabin. It sounded so tempting. Run away with an alien prince. Live happily ever after. "I don't know how I could leave the farm," I said. "If it were just me, that would be one thing, but the girls are doing well in school."

He nodded. "I understand."

He ducked his head and stepped into a smaller area that was clearly the place where he operated the ship from. It was too big to be a cockpit. The navigation console? I wasn't sure what they called it.

He sat down in a seat and gestured for me to take another one. There were four seats in total. His hands flew over the eight curved screens splayed out in front of him in a smooth arch. "Let's see what we're dealing with," he murmured.

I watched as he did his thing, presumably running diagnostics and learning the state of the ship. After a while, he leaned back. "We have some damage, but the structural integrity is solid. I'm running a self-repair sequence that will set everything right. These ships are made to take a beating, and this one did. My thrusters and shields are online." He turned one raised brow toward me. "I can fly it to your house."

I brought the snowmobile on board and he started up the ship's engine. It made a humming noise. There was a slight vibration. My gaze was glued to the windows as we rose above the trees.

"I have a lock on your home," he said. "And it's dark, so I don't think anyone will see us."

He was probably right about that. The few people who

lived out here were inside their homes this time of night, watching television or sleeping.

It took mere moments to glide to my home. His ship silently lowered in front of the red barn. He let me out to open the doors, and in no time, his sleek but somewhat battered ship, was inside and safely tucked away. It *was* a tight fit, even through the oversized doors. We closed the doors to the barn and went back onto his ship. The interior was illuminated by cool-blue lights.

We sat in the main cabin on a curved, plush sofa and took off our coats and gloves.

"Well, a spaceship is the last thing I ever expected to hide in my barn," I said with a laugh.

"A barn is the last place I ever expected to hide my ship," he said.

"And the last person I expected to share Christmas night with is a Virilian. You're basically celebrities, you know."

He looked unimpressed by this. "Celebrities who are not permitted to step foot on the planet."

"But you're here now," I said softly. We were close. I sat sideways on the couch, with my knees bumping his thigh. I placed a hand on his leg, feeling more nervous than I had, well, *ever*.

His gaze sliced to mine, then fell to my hand. His brows rose in question.

It was now or likely never. I slid my hand higher. My mouth went dry with lust. "I'm ready for more, Sakar."

His eyes were pale sapphires, narrowed to hungry slits. "How much more?"

"Everything."

He shifted toward me. "Then that is what you shall receive."

CHAPTER 9

Sakar

I dragged her onto my lap, settling her against me and groaning at the feel of her lush bottom on my rigid cock. I was hard the instant she sat beside me, but now I ached with need.

Her fingers tangled in my hair. Her mouth came on mine, hard and insistent. Nessa knew what she wanted and my desires were never in question. I sank into her, drinking in the shape and feel of her. My senses were overwhelmed with all that was Nessa.

Her hands moved over my shoulders and chest, down over my abdomen, and to my hips. I shook with need. I slid my hands up her ribs and cupped her firm breasts. She was perfect, filling my palms. I could feel her nipples harden through her clothes.

She moaned and arched her back, pressing herself more firmly into my palms. My thumbs traced taut nipples that my mouth watered to taste. I grasped the bottom of her sweater and eagerly pulled it over her head. She wore nothing underneath her sweater. I could feel the frantic beat of her heart and her shallow breath. Her skin bore an uneven flush.

Her fingers fumbled with my shirt buttons. Impatient, I pulled it over my head and tossed it away. *Where was my finesse?* Gone, along with all sensible thought.

She shifted closer. The tips of her breasts brushed my chest. I wanted this female. I wanted her now. I gathered her up in my arms and stood up.

She made a little whimper. "Where are we going?"

"To my bed," I growled.

"You have a bed in here?"

"Of course," I said. "Where else would I sleep on long journeys?" My stateroom was tiny. Most of it was taken up by a large bed. I laid her on it and covered her with my body. I pressed kisses over her skin, working my way down her trembling flesh. I dipped my tongue into her navel, then moved lower to the button of her jeans. I looked up at her. "Shall I continue?"

"Yes, please," she replied, and undid the button herself.

I pulled down her zipper. She gritted her teeth as I pulled her jeans down her hips and off her legs, along with her boots, and tossed them on the floor. Her underwear came with it. I stared down at the beauty of my mate—and I had no doubt she *was* my mate. She was exquisite. The work she did on the farm was evident in her taut muscles and sweeping curves. I put a proprietary hand on her hip. Again, the word resonated in my mind—*mine*.

I sank down and breathed in the center of her, the sweet scent of my female. She opened her legs for me and I slipped two fingers into her hot seam.

She was wet, as I knew she would be. The scent of her arousal sent me to the edge. My tail curled around her knee, lifting it and spreading her legs farther. I took in her passion-heavy eyes and parted lips. Her nostrils flared as she met my gaze with her smoldering one.

I was familiar with human anatomy. All males eligible for the match program were given an orientation on human physiology before deciding whether or not to apply. I'd never considered it. My duties came first, and there were males younger than I who deserved mates.

When I lowered my mouth to her sex, I knew the little bud in front of her opening was a pleasure zone. I flicked it with my tongue and she erupted, bucking and gasping. I held her hips in place. I inserted two fingers into her tight channel, then three, as I laved attention to her beautiful clit. Her body tightened. She went rigid and found her release.

There was a clumsy newness to the way we touched each other. Our hands were all over the place, just eager to touch and feel. It had been a long time since I'd given or received pleasure from a female. I got the sense it was the same with her. I kissed my way up her body and her hips surged up to grind against mine. Her fingers went to my pants, searching for the fastening. I brushed them aside and undid my pants. I pushed them off and I was as naked as she.

I shuddered with the effort to hold myself back. Every bit of me ached to bury my cock inside her and pound out this overwhelming desire, but I moved slowly. I settled my hips between her legs, using my tail to spread them even farther.

I kissed her deeply, wresting a whimper from her throat. My cock pressed against her sex. Her wet seam invited me inside.

I pulled my mouth away from hers and rested my forehead on her shoulder. "Are you sure?" I ground out. "Because this will change things."

"Change what?" she asked breathlessly.

"It will not be so easy to walk away," I said. "For either of us. Be sure you want this. That you want me."

Her small hands came to either side of my face. She met my gaze with her own fiery one. "I want you, Sakar. I'm so turned on I can't stand it. Take me. Take everything."

I slid my cock inside of her. Filling her. Possessing her. She was mine, now and forever. The heat of her tight sheath squeezed me. She let out a mewling noise. I checked to see if she was in discomfort, but the expression on her face was one of bliss.

I may have thought I knew what pleasure was before being with Nessa, but I was wrong. She was everything. I fucked like a male possessed, rocking my hips against her, filling her over and over, deeper, harder.

Every fiber of my being was bent on pleasuring her, and the ecstasy on her face was matched by the rapture I felt.

Her hands fisted in the sheets and her body tensed like a coiled creature. The beast inside of me roared his approval. I pumped my cock harder, bringing her to climax. I watched as she shattered, mouth opened and screaming my name. I'd never heard anything more beautiful in my life. Her pussy convulsed on my cock, squeezing me, milking me until I could barely see.

With a strangled groan, I released my seed inside of her. My arms shook. I was wrung out and my head was blank with pleasure. I rolled to my side and took her with me so we faced each other. I looked at her, stunned. Neither of us had been prepared for that.

She blinked at me in bewilderment. "What the hell, Sakar? I can't even feel my face."

I tried to chuckle but it came out as a rusty grunt. "I can't feel anything but... *Stars*. That was good."

"Understatement of the year, Virilian."

I gathered her close and pressed a kiss to her forehead. Her body went soft and I slipped my cock out of her. "We cannot sleep here. The girls may need you," I said. "As much as I would like to lie with you all night. And make love to you again and again…" I nipped her earlobe. "And again."

She groaned. "I know. It's not fair. I only get you for a short time. You have to leave in a few days. Maybe sooner, if we can find that alien creature."

I was quiet as I held my mate in my arms. I had no intention of letting her go so easily. One way or another, Nessa would be mine.

CHAPTER 10

Nessa

I woke up very early, alone in my bed. Staring at the ceiling, I thought it couldn't be possible that I'd had sex with Sakar. Surely it was a dream—too good to be true—but I wasn't imagining the subtle soreness between my legs or the loose, sumptuous feeling throughout my body. Nope, we'd done it. We'd done it *very well*.

He was down the hall, in the guest room. Ah, the temptation to sneak in and mount him was there, but I'd never act on it. I had a feeling that the more time I spent with him, the harder it would be to say goodbye. I was already dreading that moment.

I got up before everyone else, to clear the driveway and make coffee. I needed a little time to myself to think. To just process everything that had happened. The snow had stopped and the sun was out for the first time in days. It blared against the fresh snow with almost offensive brightness, making me put on sunglasses to fire up the snowblower, and clear out the driveway.

By the time I was done, the girls and Sakar were up—probably because the snowblower was loud—and all four of us worked together to clean out the animals' pens. Afterward, I let the girls check out Sakar's spaceship. For some reason, it made me nervous, but they probably wouldn't be able to see something like that again. After much oohing and aahing and questions galore, we piled into my pickup truck for another holiday tradition.

The morning after Christmas was breakfast out at Rikki's, along with half the town. I gave Sakar a fresh set of clothes, including jeans. "You're going to want to tuck that tail away," I said to him. "We're going out for breakfast."

His eyes widened. "Is that a good idea?"

"It's the only way I can think of to find out where your missing endangered species is." He looked sexy and rumpled, exactly the way someone should look after a night of great sex. My blood warmed just looking at him. I couldn't believe I'd *had* this male. Aside from being unbearably hot, Sakar was kind and loving. I could tell he genuinely liked my girls, which made me feel all soft and gushy inside about him. It also filled me with sadness. Of course, when I finally met a good guy, he had to be from another planet.

I reminded myself—for the hundredth time—that a connection and great sex did not mean we were destined to be together. We'd only known each other for a few days, under harrowing circumstances, at that.

And things weren't going to get any easier. Another phone call from the Planetary Security Agency had come through that morning while we were in the barn with the animals. They'd left a message telling me that they would be stopping by for a few quick questions in the afternoon. Meaning, *today*. So if we were going to collect Sakar's animal and get them both off of Earth, it had to be done quickly.

Mia and Violet were very excited to be going to breakfast

with our Virilian guest. They knew his alien status was a secret. We had to pretend Sakar was human, "a family friend." They felt like secret agents on a covert mission. It would've been cute if it wasn't actually a covert mission.

There was a town about forty minutes away that had big-box stores, banks, and supermarkets. But there was also our town center, which was less than ten minutes away. It had a gas station, a repair shop for every imaginable thing with an engine, and Rikki's, which sold groceries, clothes, and hardware. It *also* had a bar and diner on the premises. Yes, Rikki's took all-in-one to a new level, but lots of small towns out here had places like this.

Rikki's had decent breakfasts at a good price, if you weren't too worried about the state of your arteries. It was also the place to go to find out if an alien species was terrorizing the neighbors.

I'd walked through the doors of the diner hundreds of times, but never with nerves rising in my belly, like now. I was entering a crowded public space with a six-foot-five alien male by my side. I had done what I could to make him look human. His tail was tucked inside his jeans. I lightened the dark skin around his eyes with a little concealer, which he'd *barely* tolerated. It kind of worked. As long as no one looked too hard. It made him stand out a little less. Just a little, and he was ordered not to smile. Human men did not have fangs.

Suze, the regular waitress, greeted us with three laminated menus, which were perpetually sticky. Her gaze moved over our group and her eyes widened, along with her smile. "Oh. I see we have four today." She added another menu to her hand and grinned at the girls, sliding not-so-subtle glances at Sakar. "You two have a good Christmas?"

"Yeah, we did," said Mia, and I cringed, hoping she wouldn't spill every weird thing that had happened over the last few days. "I got the new DrakonSpell 3 video game for my system. It's so cool."

"Nice." Suze let me choose where we sat, and I picked a four-top right in the middle of the restaurant. Not that there were a lot of options. Most of the tables were taken. "How long has your guest been with you?" she asked Mia.

"Just a couple days," my daughter replied smoothly. "He's our mom's cousin, visiting from Canada."

If I had had anything in my mouth, it would've been spat everywhere. I had no idea where Mia came up with that line. And she delivered it with such deadpan that Suze could do little more than blink. There was *no way* anyone was going to believe that this gorgeous hunk of male was my cousin. It would make for a funny story in five years, but just then, all I could feel was the rising heat in my cheeks and the knowledge that this big fib of Mia's would definitely be a thing at the next PTO meeting.

Even Violet raised her brows.

"Is that so?" Suze asked, skepticism thick in her voice. She placed the four menus on the table and waggled her eyebrows at me when she thought no one was looking. "I'll give you some time with the menus and bring you girls some orange juice. Coffee for you two?" she asked Sakar and me.

"Just for me," I replied.

"Yes," Sakar said soberly. "Canadians do not like coffee."

I couldn't help but laugh this time, but Suze managed to clamp her lips together and contain a chuckle. "Got it. One coffee and three OJ's coming up."

When she stepped away, all four of us stared at each other. The people at the tables around us eyed us with speculation. Guaranteed, they'd caught part of that conversation. I sent a baffled look to Mia and mouthed, *what was that?*

She shrugged and gave me a superior look. "It's called improv, Mom."

"Where did you learn about that?" I asked.

"YouTube," she replied, and I decided I was done asking questions for now.

"Okay, everyone just look at your menus and choose something."

Sakar looked at the menu and then sent me a panicked look. He leaned toward me and said quietly in my ear, "What should I order?"

I could hear the whispers bubbling up around the tables. There was an intimacy in the tilt of his head that was decidedly *un*-cousin-like, as if anyone bought that. "The farmer's breakfast," I muttered back. It was big and had a little of everything.

"What exactly is the purpose of coming here?" he asked low enough so no one would hear.

"To listen," I whispered back. "Watch this."

I swiveled in my seat and faced Steve and Marjorie Berlik. In their late sixties, they were winding down a small dairy farm and thinking about selling to move to Florida. I put on my most charming face. "How was your Christmas?" I asked to their stunned faces. Marjorie and Steve were well-connected in town. Marjorie was on the town select board and Steve spent a lot of time here at Rikki's bar. There was little that went on that they didn't know about.

They were nice enough people, just a bit gossipy, which was exactly why I chose a table next to theirs. "It was just fine, Nessa," Steve replied. "And yours?"

"It was lovely," I replied. "Oh! How silly of me." I placed a hand on Sakar's arm and he turned in his seat. This is, um, Sam." I plastered a smile on my face and squeezed Sakar's arm. "Sam, this is Marjorie and Steve. They have a farm down not far from us."

Sakar looked immensely uncomfortable but he nodded his head. "How do you do?" he said in his low, deep voice.

I could see color rising on Marjorie's cheeks. "I do very well, thank you," she said with a slight giggle. "Did I hear correctly that you're from Canada?"

"Yes, ma'am," he replied.

"What province? Not Quebec, surely. You don't have that French accent."

I knew right then that we needed to shut off this line of questions.

"Did you lose power in the storm?" I asked. "It was quite the beast, wasn't it?"

Steve went on a bit about a couple trees that went down and a shed that had its roof collapse from the weight of the snow. Then I got to the real reason why I was talking to them. "You know, I heard something strange," I said. "Something about a crash in the woods. Might have been a meteor. Have you heard anything unusual?"

Suze returned then to take our order. "Only thing unusual I've seen is you having a very handsome Canadian cousin, Nessa." She tapped my shoulder with the back of her hand. "Honestly, where have you been hiding him? And do you have any more 'cousins' like him that you maybe want to share with the rest of us?"

She winked and I forced out a chuckle. "Nope. He's one of a kind, isn't he?"

I turned back to Steve, who held up a finger. "Actually, Mike Lark called me up to warn me to keep the cows inside for a while. Said two of his goats were eaten. Not normal eaten, I might add, but—"

"Oh, Steven, this is not pleasant breakfast conversation," Marjorie broke in.

But this was what I was here for. I scraped my chair back to turn more fully toward him and smiled. "Now I have to hear this. The Larks are one of my neighbors."

Steve ignored Marjorie's tut-tutting and went on, eyes

twinkling with the promise of gory details. "Something ate every single bit of those goats—bones, guts, and all—except for the pelt, which was damn near intact." He shook his head. "Mike Lark sent me a picture, and I couldn't believe it. Never seen anything like it in all my days."

"Can I see it?" I asked, trying not to sound too eager.

"Steve, the girl doesn't want to—" Marjorie said.

"She *asked* to see it, Mar," Steve rebutted and whipped out his phone. He showed us a picture on his phone, and it was exactly as he described. Two goat pelts, a lot of blood, and that was it.

"That is weird," I murmured.

"No joke. Mike and Laura are pretty shaken up. They're keeping the animals inside for a while. Just in case. So am I." He narrowed his eyes. "Did you say something crashed? Mike Lark said he got a call from the Planetary Security Agency." He shook his head. "Don't want those wackos in our neck of the woods."

Suze returned with our meals, and the rest of our breakfast was as uneventful as it could be, considering I was hiding a Virilian male right here in plain sight. Sakar devoured the entire farmer's breakfast and I had a feeling he would have ordered another one if he wasn't eager to be out of there.

I said hello to some other neighbors and dealt with their not-so-subtle curiosity. We almost got out of there unscathed.

As we were leaving, a couple was entering. My ex-husband with his new fiancée, the manager of the Feeds and Needs farm store that he left me for. Tiffany clung to Gavin's arm. Her expression pinched. She repositioned her hand so the new pretty diamond ring on her finger sparkled.

He stopped short at the sight of Sakar standing beside me. My heart began to pound. I didn't know why. How did I ever think Gavin was attractive? I took in his small, unkind eyes and the straggly beard that he tried to grow. He had a nice physique, I supposed, but it was nothing compared to Sakar's magnificence. Anyone with eyes could see which was the superior male. The problem was, if anyone could see through my little farce, it was Gavin. He knew damn well I didn't have any Canadian cousins. My ex's eyes narrowed. "Morning, Ness."

"Merry Christmas, Gavin. Tiffany," I gritted out.

The girls were silent. There was no love lost between them and my ex. They were solidly Team Mom, which was gratifying, but Mia was outspoken enough to make this run-in far more uncomfortable than it needed to be.

I felt Sakar's hand on my back. "Tell me *this* isn't the male who—" Oh good god, he infused enough scorn in that cut-off sentence to make me cringe.

"We're on our way out," I said quickly, cutting him off. "Goodbye." I shifted toward my truck, but Gavin didn't budge.

"Who the fuck are you?" Gavin asked, hackles up.

"Don't swear in front of my children," I snarled. "Sak—ah, Sam, this is Gavin. My ex."

Sakar let out a snort. "For good reason," he muttered, loud enough for all of us to hear him.

Tiffany looked like she had a lemon wedge in her mouth. "Let's just go, Gav."

"No." Gavin dug in his heels. "Who does this asshole think he is?"

Sakar actually laughed. "I think I'm *not* the fool who left her."

Gavin's face turned an unpleasant shade of red. "Trust me. She's no prize," he sneered.

"She's a treasure." Sakar closed the distance between them. In a flash, his hand gripped the front of Gavin's shirt and jerked him forward. He bared his teeth, revealing the fangs he was *supposed* to keep hidden. "You will speak respectfully to Nessa and her children."

"Or what?" Gavin squeaked out.

Sakar's smile went cold. He tilted his head. "Oh, I could go into detail about what I would do to you, small human, but it would ruin your breakfast." He dropped Gavin and pushed him away as if it disgusted him to be near him.

The color drained from Gavin's face. "*What* are you?"

"Nessa's cousin," Sakar replied smoothly. "From Canada."

Tiffany all but dragged Gavin into Rikki's. She sent a look of pure venom over her shoulder as she propelled her visibly shaken fiancé into the diner.

CHAPTER 11

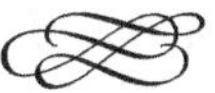

Nessa

"Well, I'll have to find a new place to buy feed from," I said wryly. "Way to act human."

"He was disrespecting you and your children," said Sakar. "He got away lightly."

Violet beamed at Sakar. "That was *awesome*."

Sakar raised one brow. "Unpleasant man."

"Let's get out of here." I grabbed his sleeve and pulled him toward my truck.

"That was the coolest thing I've ever seen," said Violet. "I've wanted to make him feel bad for what he did for so long." She turned adoring eyes up to Sakar. "Did you see his face? I think he peed himself a little."

Sakar smirked and got in the truck. "That would be gratifying."

"Moving on." I had to admit, hearing Gavin say out loud that I was no prize had not felt good. But Sakar hadn't blinked. He'd defended me instantly. "Well, at least we got what we needed," I said. "It sounds like the *daerli* we're looking for found a meal at the Lark farm, which is adjacent to my woods. We've got to find it quickly, before Planetary Security shows up later today."

Sakar's eyes narrowed. "You didn't tell me this."

"No point in it," I said. "How hungry would this *daerli* be after eating two goats?"

Sakar frowned. "How big are these goats?"

"About that size." I pointed out the window. We were actually passing the Lark farm. Their small herd of milking goats were in their outside pen with Mike as he cleared it of snow.

"I think the *daerli* would be satiated with two of those for quite some time," he said. "But he would be scared and would not react well if a human came upon him."

I remembered my run-in with the *daerli* and I could imagine just how poorly that would go. The *daerli* was a terrifying-looking creature. Any rational human would reach for a weapon when faced with those fangs and claws. No one would give it the benefit of the doubt.

We got home and pulled into the garage.

"So what are we doing now?" Mia asked.

"You and your sister are going to go inside the house and lock the door. Sakar and I are going to find his missing *daerli*."

"Oh," Mia whined. "We want to go, too."

"Out of the question." I put on my serious-mom face. "You two will stay in the house where it's safe. This creature might be scared and dangerous."

They both turned pleading eyes to Sakar, but he shook his head. "Your mother is correct. You heard what happened to the goats."

Mia scrunched up her face. "Those poor goats."

The girls got out of the truck and—grumbling—went inside as Sakar and I prepared to leave again. I threw a couple tarps in the pickup's bed and opened the door to the extra refrigerator I kept in the garage for animal medicine and spare gallons of milk. On the door was a syringe of sedative that had been meant for Prince Charming six months ago when he'd gotten an infection in his hoof. I'd kept it just in case.

"The *daerli* will not fit on that vehicle we took to get to my ship last night," he said. "How do you propose we move through the snow?"

"We're taking the truck," I said. "We're going to the Lark farm."

Sakar's eyes widened. "We're going there and asking them if they have a *daerli* hiding in their barn?"

"No. According to Steve Berlik, the Larks got a call from the Planetary Security Agency, too. I'm going to stop in and talk to him about that. You are going to find your *daerli* and get him in the back of the truck."

Sakar looked at me like I was out of my mind. "What makes you think the *daerli* will come to me like a docile cow?"

"I saw the way you were with him right after the crash. If it hadn't been for that explosion, he would've come with you. If you need help, inject him with this." I handed him the capped syringe. "It's just a sedative. It should keep him calm, if it has the same effect as it does on horses."

He sat there, rigid and frowning. "I think you're overestimating my skills with this creature."

"I'm not. They're coming *today*, Sakar," I said. "There will be agents swarming this town, talking to everyone. They *will* find a crashed alien ship, with dead aliens, in the woods. *My* woods. You've got to find this *daerli* and get both of you out of here."

"Nessa..." His voice sounded choked with longing. His gaze was hungry. "We must talk about last night. About us."

My heart squeezed. "Last night was wonderful. It was amazing and I… I felt things." I reached out and took one of his large hands in both of mine. "But you're an alien who's not allowed to be here. I wish you could stay and we could see where this might go, but…" I trailed off and dropped my gaze. "We both know it's impossible."

His hand turned over and he squeezed both of mine. "Nothing is impossible. I will find a way."

"Short of both of us joining the match program, and getting miraculously matched by one of your sages, I don't see how." I smiled sadly. "I'm too old to be accepted, anyway."

"I'm older than you," he said. "And I don't give a damn about your age," he said. "I want you. And your amazing children."

Tears came to my eyes. Did he have to be so perfect? Did he have to be exactly the guy I never thought would turn in my direction? I turned on the truck ignition and the old truck rumbled to life.

"Let's just catch this *daerli*, okay? We'll leave the future of our relationship to another time."

I drove down the road to the Lark farm, which was about a mile away.

Sakar was ducked down so if the Larks looked outside, they'd only see me getting out of the pickup truck. I went up to their door and knocked. Laura Lark opened the door. She looked shaken and beckoned me inside. "Are you here because of the call?"

I opened my eyes wide. "Did you get one too?"

"Mike!" Laura bellowed throughout the house. "Nessa's here. She got a call from that agency too."

My goal here was to keep them occupied as long as I possibly could so that Sakar could find the *daerli* and get it into the truck. I managed to finagle a cup of tea that I didn't really want, and an invitation to the kitchen table, where I slowly worked through a piece of mince pie and some chocolate chip cookies.

I was getting way too good at lying to my neighbors, I thought, as I told them the girls had heard something, but we didn't know what it was and I hadn't given it much thought. Laura and Mike were not thrilled with the idea of the Planetary Defense agents coming here and going through everything. I couldn't argue with that, although my reasons were different from theirs.

They were nervous about aliens potentially being in the area and eating their goats. I was worried that the alien I was harboring would be found. I managed to stay there for an hour and change before it became awkward and I knew I had to leave. I only hoped that Sakar had been successful.

I said my goodbyes and promised to let them know what the agents said to me when they visited. I walked back to my truck with a lump in my throat. I glanced at the truck bed and saw an enormous lump in the back, under the two tarps. Sakar was nowhere to be seen. Laura and Mike stood on their porch waving at me.

I had no choice. I got in and drove home with a sick feeling in my belly. I'd come back later and find him, but if that was the *daerli* in the back of my truck, I needed to get it out of here.

I parked in front of the red barn and held my breath as I pulled up the edge of the tarps. I saw a black shaggy pelt and staggered back with a gasp. *He'd done it.* He'd gotten the *daerli* sedated and in the truck bed. The tarps moved and shifted. I staggered backward, terror in my throat, only to see a familiar, tawny head emerge, followed by the rest of him. Sakar grinned at me. "Success," he said triumphantly.

My knees almost collapsed in relief. "Thank goodness. Let's get him in your spaceship right now."

But then, the *daerli* stood up and shook like a dog in the

rain. I pointed, finger trembling. "Oh no. It's waking up. It's—"

"He was never asleep," Sakar said gently. He placed a hand on the *daerli's* head and the beast leaned into his touch with a noise that sounded like a purring cat but a lot louder. The *daerli* leaped out of the truck and came up to me, sniffing.

"You were right. I could handle him. He's not vicious," said Sakar. "When you met him, he was terrified and he had not been treated well by the Shaax—the aliens who were transporting him."

I held perfectly still. Sweat dripped down my back as the *daerli* sniffed me from head to toe and then back up again, before opening his massive mouth and licking the side of my head. "Oh, ew," I gurgled out, before seeing narrow black eyes blinking curiously at me.

"Mom." Violet and Mia stood outside the house, gawking at the massive doglike creature. Before I could yell at them to get back in the house, Mia streaked down the path through the snow. Violet reached out to grab her, but Mia was too fast.

It felt like it happened in slow motion. Her arms were out. A huge smile was on her face. The *daerli* immediately tensed at the sudden rush of a new person. He arched his back and showed his teeth. Mia wasn't seeing this. She must have seen him lick me and didn't see the danger she was running directly into.

A scream coiled in my throat. I lunged forward, but I was too far away, too slow. I watched in horror as Mia got closer.

Sakar, moving faster than I thought possible, swung in front of Mia and scooped her off the ground. He held her tight in his arms and dropped to one knee. He angled his body and held out a hand to the *daerli* just as he was about to charge.

The *daerli* skidded to an awkward stop, pressing his nose to Sakar's hand.

Relief almost made me collapse. I was pretty sure *I* peed a little.

The *daerli's* fur smoothed out. The aggression disappeared. He sat on his haunches and sniffed Mia's leg curiously.

Mia sat quietly in Sakar's arms. My knees went rubbery as I stumbled toward them. I saw him murmuring something in her ear.

She nodded and wiped tears off her cheek.

Violet was crying on the step. "Is Mia okay?" she called out.

"Yes, everyone is fine," said Sakar. He rose, still holding Mia, cradled in his huge arms. He strode over to me and placed her down. My youngest daughter immediately wound her arms around my middle and squeezed. I held her and kissed the top of her head. "My sweet girl," I whispered. "Please. Don't do that again. I was so…" I couldn't even finish the sentence. I just hugged her.

Sakar beckoned Violet to come toward us. "Walk slowly," he said. "It is always wise to approach an unknown creature gently, so they do not perceive you as a threat."

Violet did it perfectly. She approached the *daerli* as she would a strange dog, keeping her eyes averted and coming in slowly. When she got close, Sakar put an arm around her shoulders and showed her how to greet the *daerli*. He gently sniffed her and then nudged her hand for some pets.

Mia uncurled herself from me and joined them. Soon, the *daerli* had put both of them into giggles as he licked them and then rolled onto his back for belly scratches.

Sakar came to stand by my side.

"Thank you," I said shakily. "You saved her life."

"I would never allow harm to come to your children." He turned crystal blue eyes to mine. "I would die first."

The last remaining walls around my heart shattered like glass and crumbled to dust. "Oh, Sakar." My voice broke over his name.

He looked to the girls with a muscle pulsing in his jaw. "I told her that the *daerli* is not vicious, but he is a predator and would defend himself."

"How do you have this way with this creature?"

He shrugged. "I've worked with unique species for quite some time," he said. "The *daerli* is not a mindless beast, but a creature with thoughts and opinions. He wants to get out of here and be someplace safe."

"So do you." I looked into his eyes. "Whether you admit it or not."

"I do want that," he said. "Being in that public restaurant, I know that I do not fit here. But I do not wish to leave you."

I leaned up and pressed my mouth to his. I kissed him, right there. Mia and Violet could see me and that was okay. "I don't wish you to leave us, either."

His hands spanned my waist. "Nessa, there must be a—"

"Everyone freeze," said a voice through a megaphone. "Let us see your hands."

I spun to see at least two dozen armed agents positioned around my front yard with weapons aimed at us. The *daerli* moved in front of Mia and Violet and growled.

So much for arriving this afternoon. The Planetary Security Agency was here, *now*.

CHAPTER 12

Sakar

Heat crept under my skin. It moved through my veins like magma. It was the sight of those agents with their weapons drawn and pointed at my mate and her children that did it.

Protective instincts expanded inside of me. "They won't shoot."

"How do you know?" Nessa asked in a high-pitched voice.

"Because they don't wish to damage relations between our two species." I said that part loud enough for the agents to hear.

They didn't say anything, but I knew it was true. Earthlings gained a great deal from their relationship with Virilians. They weren't going to shoot, but they did want to capture me.

I slowly raised my hands. "Get everyone into the red barn and onto my ship," I said quietly to Nessa.

"Back off," Nessa called out to the agents. "This is Prince

Sakar of Virilia. He crashed here and hasn't harmed us. He's peaceful."

The agents didn't look impressed. Plus, "peaceful" was a hard claim to make considering what I would look like in a short time. I could feel the change sliding through me. Primal state was something only talked about, but a few experienced the change from normal Virilian to fiery demon warrior for themselves.

"I won't let them take you and the girls," I said through my teeth. "And you can't be near me right now."

"Why not?" Her hand gripped the back of my shirt. "What are you talking about, Sakar?"

I turned my eyes slowly to meet hers. My vision was tinted red and I knew it wasn't from fear or anger. The boiling in my blood was not a metaphor. I met her gaze and her brow furrowed. "What's going on with your—"

"Nessa," I said as gently as I could, "get everyone onto the ship."

She stared, transfixed by my eyes, which I knew weren't blue anymore. My forearms bulged with thick, red veinlike markings.

Nessa released my shirt and stepped back. "You're so hot. Wh-what's happening to you?"

"My body and soul are preparing to protect my mate," I said. "I love you, Nessa. If you trust nothing else, trust this."

Before she could respond, the agent in front, who wore a gray uniform and a funny little hat, spoke into his voice projector device again. "Everyone stay still," he said. "No one has to get hurt."

"The only one who might get hurt is you, if you make one move to touch any of these females," I said, then turned fiery red eyes to Nessa. "Go," I ordered her. "Please." I wished I could touch her, but I was becoming too hot. The primal form was taking hold of me, drawing up an ancient shift that Virilians rarely experienced any longer.

This time, she backed away, drawing her children into her arms and slowly stepping back. Even the *daerli* went with her, proving he was more intelligent than most would think. He positioned himself in front of the females, head down and eyes sharp. He was probably a little afraid of me, too. I would be. I looked very different than I had a short time ago.

"Stop walking, ma'am," the agent called out. "I don't want to hurt you."

My primal form did not like that. Heat flared out of me. My head hurt and the smell of burning clothes filled my nostrils as my body heat incinerated the shirt and pants Nessa had given me. All I wore now were the fireproof leather pants. My tail was free, having changed from blue to crimson. It swung back and forth, tipped with a lethal scorching barb.

A murmur of unease went through the agents. A Virilian's primal form was terrifying and very dangerous. I could feel the large, curving flame horns flickering over my head. My body expanded, growing a bit larger. My muscles enlarged and flooded with strength. I was ready for battle, according to my body.

I didn't know what Nessa and the others were doing behind me. But I heard the creak of the barn door rolling open.

They will be safe on my ship. None of the weapons these humans held could breach the armored hull. And now, those weapons wouldn't affect me either. My skin was molten armor. It was the closest I would ever come to being invincible.

I took a step toward the agents, and then another. The snow around me was melting quickly. It made sizzling puddles at my feet and filled the air around me with steamy fog.

The agents shifted back. Panic flared in more than one pair of eyes. Fear must have made one of them crack and an agent fired their weapon. The projectile struck me in the thigh. It had all the impact of a snowball against a rock wall. A few more shots were fired before their leader snarled at them to cease.

"We don't want trouble," he called out. "We just want to talk."

"You might've thought about that before you showed up with your weapons drawn," I said. "Threatening my mate and her family."

"Your mate?" the agent said. "We have no records of anyone in the Virilian match program living in these parts."

"She is not in the match program. But she is, nevertheless, mine."

"What about that creature?" he asked.

"The creature does not belong here," I replied. "I'm taking it home."

"You're not bringing anything anywhere," said a new voice. A large man strode to the front, thumbs hooked in his pants pockets. He had a hard look. I could tell instantly that he did not like my kind. I also knew there would be no discussion with this one. "General Robert Mason of the InterPlanetary Security Agency. You are relieved, agent," he said to the man I'd been speaking with.

This agency clearly outranked the Planetary Security Agency. How many agencies did Earth need to defend itself from aliens who didn't even *want* their planet?

"Now, you tell the humans and that abomination you have with you to come out and this will be over quickly," Mason said. "No one needs to get hurt."

I lowered my arms. My thoughts were not as articulate as

they had been. Primal state unraveled some of our more civilized traits. "You will not touch her," I growled out.

"You have *no* rights here, Virilian," said Mason. "Your very presence is illegal according to statute 88.5 of the Interplanetary Code of Alien Relations. You can turn yourself into fire, ice, or rock itself, and I will still take you in for illegal trespass onto planet Earth. Let's add on brainwashing and possible assault on a human woman and her children. They'll be examined by our medical professionals and held in quarantine for six months."

"I would die before I allowed harm to come to them."

"We'll see what the interplanetary judges say." He crossed his arms. "And I don't care if they shut down the match program. Would be the best thing, if you ask me." The other agent—the one whom I'd been speaking with before this fool turned up—slanted him a look, but stayed silent.

No, there would be no discussion with this male. I would have to do something Nessa wouldn't want me to do. I could only hope she'd forgive me later.

Among the bands around my wrist was a thick silver one—my link to my ship. I pressed my thumb to the top of it. Even in primal state, it accepted my command. I closed my fiery eyes as the familiar hum started up. My ship was activated. I was sending Nessa, her children, and the *daerli* to Virilia without me. I was stranding myself in the process, but I didn't care.

Nessa and her children were my family. I threw my head back and released a primal bellow as the top of the barn exploded and my ship blotted out the sun. For a second, all eyes turned from me to the ship, which blasted off with hardly a sound and winked out of sight.

I crossed my arms, missing Nessa already and feeling extremely cross with these men. "So. What would you like to discuss?"

CHAPTER 13

Nessa

I knew what was happening, but I still didn't believe it. The ship moved and vibrated the same way it had when Sakar had started it up to move it from the forest to the barn. Only this time, it didn't have a pilot. I dashed back to the door, but of course, it was sealed.

I held out my hands. "Did anybody touch anything?"

Mia and Violet froze and turned to me. Neither of them was near a screen or instrument. No one had entered the little room with all the screens and consoles. We were all in the main cabin. It looked the same as it had when I was here last, making out with Sakar on the couch.

"No," said Violet, who had turned a pale shade of ash. "Neither of us touched anything."

The *daerli* looked confused too. He paced the cabin, letting out a trilling sort of whine. Mia went over to him and patted him. "It's okay," she soothed. "I'm sure Sakar will be here soon."

Unless Sakar could beam himself up here, like a real Star

Trek person, he wasn't going to be meeting us here. There were screens in the main cabin, but everything was in Virilian. I was afraid to touch anything in the cockpit room, but it was plain to see out the windows that we had left our home planet and were in space.

"Where are we going?" Violet asked.

I looked at her hopelessly. "I don't know."

"Virilia," said Mia. "That's where we're going."

Violet and I stared at her. "How do you know?"

She pointed to a screen on the far wall. It was covered in symbols I didn't understand. "See? It is right here." She tapped the screen. It turned red and Mia whipped her hand away. The screen went back to normal. "That word means Virilia, so that's probably where we're going."

I gaped at her for a moment, before shaking my head. "How do you know what that says?"

She shook her head. "YouTube. There are people who are really into Virilian culture and know their language and stuff," she said as if it were also obvious. "They do language tutorials and that's the word for Virilia in Sakar's language."

"And all those other symbols are probably the distance and the trajectory and speed, and all of those things." I sounded ignorant, but I wasn't a space traveler. I wished more than anything that I could give my children some more reassurance, but here I was, taking comfort in the knowledge that an eight-year-old got from YouTube videos.

Violet sent me a serious look. "I bet you're glad you let her watch YouTube."

"Oh, yeah," I moaned. "I'm mother of the year."

"Did Sakar send us away on this ship?" Mia asked, eyes wide.

There were some things YouTube could *not* explain. I beckoned her over and gathered her on my lap. She nestled her head in my neck and I held her tight. Violet sat next to me and I wrapped my other arm around her. "I don't know for sure, but I think he put us on his ship and sent us away to keep us safe from the people with guns."

"Why did he look like that?" Violet wanted to know. "He looked like a—a demon."

I shuddered to think about it. "I'm not sure," I replied.

"That's his primal form," said Mia, muffled at my neck.

I pried her out and met her gaze. "His what?"

She rolled her eyes. "Mom, seriously, don't you know anything? When Virilian guys feel like their wives or families are threatened, they get all hot and grow fire horns. It's *really* rare." She said the last part as if talking about a hard-to-find Pokémon card.

"You know a lot about the Virilians," I said. "Why do you watch so much on them?" I was almost afraid of the answer.

Mia shrugged one shoulder. "They come from space, which is really cool. And they have tails."

"Yes, they do," I murmured, remembering how Sakar's had been quite effective at spreading my legs. "It only happens when a Virilian is protecting his family, huh?"

Mia nodded. "Does that mean Sakar thinks we're his family?"

Violet frowned at this. "Probably not," she said. "He was probably protecting himself and the *daerli*."

Mia shook her head and laughed. "Vi, the *daerli* is not his wife."

"Well, men don't stay with us," Violet said in a rush, arms crossed and shoulders up around her ears. "Dad died and Gavin left."

I placed a hand on the back of my oldest daughter's head. She was too young to be so hardened. "It wasn't dad's fault that he passed away. And Gavin, well, we'll talk about him someday, but our paths weren't meant to stay together," I said gently. "Two men caused you pain, but remember that the choices of one and fate of the other don't represent *all* of them."

Violet's green gaze—the same shade as mine—probed my eyes. "What about Sakar?"

I sighed. "Considering we're currently not even, or very soon won't be, in the same solar system, I can't answer that."

"You like him, though."

"I like him a lot. What do *you* think of him?"

"I like him," Mia piped in.

"I like him, too," said Violet. "And if he's willing to strand himself on Earth with all of those agents with guns who want to lock him up, he must care about us a lot."

My gaze went unfocused, so I stared at the wall. "I guess he…must."

And maybe I did, too.

The passing of time was impossible to tell. Out the window, it was black. Mia's knowledge of the Virilian language pretty much ended with that word, so we didn't know how long we would be in space or, even, *for sure* where we were going.

All four of us slept in Sakar's bed—where I had some very dirty memories—including the *daerli,* which Mia named Axel. He was clearly enamored with her.

We found food and water in some of the containers and storage units. We also encountered some scary-looking weapons, which we did not touch. Occasionally, messages would appear on the screen and a disembodied voice would announce something, but no one understood what was said. We all hoped it was nothing important.

And as nothing important continued to happen, we began to relax and even have a little fun. The view outside was magnificent. I *did* worry about my animals and hoped that one of our neighbors would stop by and tend to them. I couldn't even imagine what everyone back on Earth thought happened to us. Abducted? Run away with an alien?

The farther we went from Earth, the more my problems felt far away. I'd probably been fired from my medical transcription job. There might be an amber alert out for my children, and by now, the other crashed ship with the alien bodies had probably been found. The thought of returning to Earth seemed like a chaotic shitshow.

How did someone go back to a mundane existence after this?

CHAPTER 14

Sakar

I was not interested in a fight. With Nessa, her children, and the *daerli* safely on their way to Virilia, I had nothing to fight for and had enough sense about me to know that the consequences would be disastrous if I obliterated the human forces here.

I sat down on the cold ground and waited, breathing through the battle instincts and adrenaline that pumped through my engorged veins. "I am not familiar with your agency," I said.

"It's a new one," he replied. "Secret, unless we're needed, and we don't take any shit from aliens."

I nearly laughed. This was the most absurd thing I could think of anyone saying to a Virilian male in full primal state. An excellent way to get himself killed. If I was so inclined, I merely had to touch him to burn the skin right off his bones. I thought of Nessa, Violet, and Mia, and the consequences for them if I acted out. "I will speak with a designated

Virilian envoy and no one else." I pinned the annoying General Mason with my flaming gaze. "Definitely not you."

He didn't care for that. He immediately began peppering me with questions. I pretended I didn't hear them and set my mind elsewhere. I yawned as his questions turned into threats that grew more and more gruesome. I listened to the steam sizzle around me as my molten hot body continue to melt the snow around me.

At one point Mason ordered agents to shoot me again, but they wisely refused. At last, the angry general left and the original agent walked up to me.

"I will call an envoy," he said quietly. "But can you just tell me, is the woman and her children safe?"

I met his gaze with a quiet smile. "Now, finally an intelligent question." I nodded. "Yes, they are."

He closed his eyes. The tension went out of his shoulders. "Okay."

"What is your name?" I asked.

"Peterson," he replied. "Agent Peterson. I followed orders back then, to surround and apprehend you." He shook his head. "I shouldn't have followed them."

"The orders make sense," I replied. "If you were apprehending a criminal, you would have been in the right. But Virilians have no design on your planet. We are not your enemy."

"I never thought you were." He shook his head. "I am sorry about this."

I sighed. "Me, too. I do not like being separated from my mate."

He winced. The other agents were no longer tense with guns aimed, either. Still, I could hear the sound of many of their helicopters in the distance.

"I am very curious to see what your people think they will do with me," I said.

Peterson looked over my oversized red, flaming body. "How long will you stay this way?"

I shrugged. "It's different for everyone."

"Well, looks like we're gonna be here for a while. Is there anything I can do for you, Prince Sakar?"

I stretched out my legs. I couldn't feel the cold coming off the ground or the chill air. "You can get a message to my cousin, King of Tagja City, on Virilia. Tell him that my mate and her children, and the male *daerli* he wanted rescued from the black market, will be arriving in his shuttle bay soon."

The agent's face opened in surprise. "Your cousin is a king?"

I nodded. "Hence why I am a prince."

"Oh shit." He rubbed his hands over his face.

"Don't worry, Peterson. Virilians are not the retaliatory type."

He shook his head. "I wish I could say the same for humans."

"Give yourself a few thousand more years," I said with a smile. "Your society will get there."

I sat there for days with guards around, keeping an eye on me and holding back the many curious people who wanted to see the Virilian. News organizations caught wind of me, which gave the agents and the military even more of a headache. Drones buzzed in the air and reporters tried to sneak in to see me.

I couldn't have cared less. There was no place for me to go. I would damage or destroy any vehicle they put me on. I could not be in proximity to anything flammable. Honestly, Nessa's frozen front yard wasn't the worst place for me in my current state. My body still pumped with chemicals that made me ready for a fight. The humans suggested building a metal enclosure around me, but I asked that they refrain from doing that. Enclosing a Virilian in a small space all but ensured that the beast would win and I would tear it down.

I was still engorged with the urge to fight, but mentally, I was just tired. I wanted Nessa back, I wanted to go home, and I wanted people to stop asking me the same questions over and over again.

I must have recounted my chase with the Shaax aliens fifteen times. Of course, I wouldn't answer anything until the agency promised that Nessa's animals would be cared for. I wouldn't have them starve to death in that barn while agents sifted through her house. Peaches and Prince Charming deserved better. Agents even collected the eggs.

It was several Earth days later when I received the message I had been hoping for. Agent Peterson came up to me with a paper in his hand. "For you." He held it out to me.

I raised one eyebrow. "I can't take it. Could you read it please?"

"Ah, of course." He unsealed the envelope, color rising on his cheeks. "It is a message from King Virak of Tagja City to you. It reads, *I hope this finds you well, cousin. Nessa Thompson and her children are well and enjoying the company of the human women of our city, including my mate. She expresses concern for the animals in her barn and hopes they are being tended to. The two young females are utterly charming. The younger one is quite attached to the male* daerli *and has assigned him a name. As for the* daerli, *the female has accepted him. I am hopeful for pups. Your release has been arranged. We are also undergoing a full reconsideration of human-Virilian relations. To that end, I have named you my ambassador so that you may travel freely to both Earth and Virilia. Talks will commence after you have returned to your usual state and have spent some time reuniting with your family. I am sending a ship to collect you. Best regards, Virak.*"

Peterson smiled widely. "I suppose you are free to go."

I laughed, more than pleased with my cousin's message. "I

was free to go at any time." I raised a hand, red and bulging with dark veins. "Who would stop me?"

Peterson chuckled back. "True. But we both know you still can't go anywhere."

I lay back on the ground and gazed up at the clear blue sky. Far, far away, up there, my mate was on my home planet. "Soon, my love."

CHAPTER 15

Nessa

I hadn't known what to expect of Virilia. When the ship landed on a large, enclosed landing bay and lowered underground, we were all alarmed. I didn't know what was going on, and until the ship's hatch opened and the ramp lowered, I still wasn't one hundred percent sure we were going to Virilia.

We descended the metal ramp slowly. Mia was wrapped around me so tightly, we must have looked like one person staggering down the ramp. Glued to her side was Axel, the *daerli*. Violet was trying hard to be brave and stand on her own, but she gripped my hand hard.

A group of several dozen had assembled to greet us. Virilians dressed in colorful, formal clothing stood there, but my gaze latched onto some grinning humans.

A woman with long black hair stepped forward. She wore a dark blue jumpsuit with a simple silver circlet around her head. Beside her stood a tall, somewhat severe male. "Welcome, Nessa, Mia, and Violet." She smiled and I immediately felt at ease. "I am Jessa Braal, queen of Tagja City. This is my mate, King Virak. We welcome you, even though the circumstances could be better."

A laugh gurgled out of me. "Thank you," I said with relief. "I guess Sakar managed to get a message here?"

"Oh, he did indeed, Nessa," said Virak. "I had a great deal to say to the human authorities on your planet regarding their treatment of you all."

"I still can't wrap my head around it. Is Sakar okay?" I asked anxiously.

He nodded. "Sakar is currently invincible in his primal form and will be released as soon as he's back to his usual state." He swept his arms wide. "These are some of our advisors, friends, and local officials. We're all here to make you comfortable during your stay." The king's gaze moved to my kids and his eyes twinkled. "We have so much to show you. It will be wonderful to have more children here."

Mia eased away from me. Her hand was fisted in Axel's fur. "Is this a safe place for Axel?" Nothing like confronting a king immediately upon meeting him.

Virak smiled. "Not only is it safe, but there's another one of his kind here. A female." He waggled his eyebrows. "So, hopefully he'll have a girlfriend."

Mia nodded. "Good. He needs someone to talk to other than me."

Jessa smiled up at her mate. She looked very happy and healthy here, and she fit in with the Virilians. There were plenty of blue, spiked tails in this group.

"Please come with us." Jessa beckoned us toward a hallway on the other side of the hangar. "I'll show you to your quarters, and give you a tour of the city. You can go anywhere you like, but I'm sure you'd like to know where you'll be sleeping, and maybe get a proper meal and a shower."

All of those things sounded wonderful, not that the provisions on Sakar's ship weren't edible.

Violet's hand unclenched from mine. She looked up at me with bright twinkling eyes. We walked through the massive corridor, decorated with sculptures and paintings. "This place is awesome," she said in a fierce whisper.

It was. The instant we stepped into Tagja City, every worry I had vanished. It was a marvel, carved from stone. It looked ancient, but nothing had fallen to ruin. Fresh water trickled through streams cut into the floor. There was light, despite being underground, and plants, flowers. The air was clear and sweet. Mia danced around pointing things out, staring in obvious delight. My chest tightened a little bit. Would they *want* to go home after this? After being on an alien planet, would Earth be enough for them?

Would it be enough for me?

For about three weeks—Earth time—I contemplated this question. I became good friends with Jessa and the other human women who had stayed on Virilia with their children and mates.

There was so much to do, and see. King Virak's menagerie alone was spectacular. He gave me and the girls a tour personally. The tall, serious-looking Virilian, who did not look like the type to crack a smile very often, transformed into soft adoration in the presence of his mate in the habitats he made for the creatures he rescued. He and Jessa were natural together and loved each other very much. That was obvious. Just as obvious was the love they had for their two small children. With blue, barbed tails and sharp eye teeth, it would be easy to forget they had a human mother. The bright, happy children rushed to her arms and locked their small arms around her neck.

They had much to show us in the menagerie, too. Mia supervised the introduction of Axel to the female *daerli*. To say it was love at first sight was putting it mildly. The female *daerli* looked exactly like Axel, just a little smaller. The two made trilling, purring noises at each other, and then disappeared into the enclosure's vegetation.

The menagerie was enormous. Paths wound through what was almost a jungle, complete with massive trees, streams, and little ponds. Everywhere I looked, unique creatures chased each other through the trees, flew with vividly colored wings, or peered out from secluded places, blinking at us with big, luminous eyes. Virak looked very proud of it.

"How long did it take you to build all this?" I asked as Mia and Violet darted off down the paths to see all the creatures.

"I have lost track of the time, to be honest," he said. "I am still working on it. There are still new chambers and new habitats I would like to make for some of the more specialized species. The *daerli* you so kindly brought back with you is native to this very planet. It's my hope that eventually, we can get enough breeding pairs to reintroduce them to the mountainous region of Berakan. We all must find habitats we are best suited for." He inclined his head. "Just like you and Sakar."

Jessa turned her knowing eyes to me. "Have you thought about where you will primarily live?"

My head went blank. "Um...we haven't talked about anything even close."

"He turned into his primal form for you," she said. "He loves you, and I have a feeling you feel the same."

"As I said to him, it would be easier if it were just me, but I've got my girls to think of. Moving to another town is one thing. To another planet is another thing entirely. I want to make sure they can make choices and have options."

"And everything feels really complicated right now." Jessa smiled and hooked her arm through mine. "I have a feeling things will work out."

"It will work out if I must journey to Earth myself and speak some sense into your planet's leaders," said Virak. "If anyone deserves happiness, it is my cousin. He's fought in wars for too long. He's been alone for too long."

I had been open with both of them about how I met Sakar, and how far our relationship progressed. My girls also knew I had feelings for Sakar—it was obvious. I also knew they liked him. But was it enough for a serious commitment?

After three weeks, though, Mia and Violet were talking about school, their friends, and what they were missing on Earth. Violet was worried about how much homework she would have to make up. Math was hard for her and she worried about falling behind. When I asked them if they wanted to go home, they said they did, but they also liked it here. We were all learning Virilian and were accepted in this place.

I didn't know what I expected to feel when Jessa showed up excitedly at our door, letting us know that Sakar had just landed. He was *here*. His body was back to normal and he was asking for us. The girls were somewhere else—probably in the menagerie—but I ran into them on the way to the hangar. Someone had told them the news, too. We rushed together, through the corridors that were now well-known to us.

I dashed through the entrance to the hangar where all the ships were kept. There, across the way, I saw him. Same shaggy, tawny hair. Same snug brown pants. Markings on his chest and arms were a little different now. More sinuous. More resembling flames. But the fiery horns were gone and so were the red veins.

He looked like him again. I dashed toward him, feet slapping against the stone floor. He turned. Bright blue eyes widened, then his arms opened and I was in them. He hugged me close to him, burying his face in my neck.

"Nessa," he breathed against my skin. His hands were like brands against my back. He leaned back enough to kiss me, deep and hard, before stepping back and turning his gaze to Mia and Violet, who were right behind me. He opened his arms to them, too, and we held each other close. Like a family.

"I missed you both so much," he said to them.

The moment I saw the look in my girls' eyes, I knew I would not be leaving this male. There was enough here. Enough love. Enough everything. We would make a family together.

"I am so sorry." His gaze probed mine. "My only thought was to get you someplace safe. I didn't mean to send you here without telling you. I found it shockingly hard to get messages to Virilia from your planet without going through an enormous amount of permissions and forms…which I was unable to sign, being that I set anything I touched on fire."

I cupped his face in my hands. "It's okay. We're safe and your people have been more than welcoming. It has been incredible for the three of us and I'm so glad you're back here safe." My brow lowered as worries descended. "Did they treat you horribly? Please tell me they didn't hurt you."

He chuckled and shook his head. "I can't be hurt in the primal form. The only thing they could do was leave me alone. I wouldn't answer any questions until your animals were cared for."

Tears sprung to my eyes. "You are so damn amazing. I love you, Sakar."

"I love you, too, Nessa."

"Are you guys going to get married?" Violet asked, eyes narrowed.

"It would be my honor to marry your mother," said Sakar. "As her daughters, what would the two of you think of that?"

Violet stared him down for long moments, before replying, "I would be okay with it."

I managed not to react to that resounding endorsement from Violet.

"So would I," Mia piped up. "You're going to say yes, right, Mom?"

My heart lifted, along with my arms, which wound around my mate's neck. "Yes," I replied, and I kissed him with all the love I had in my heart.

CHAPTER 16

Nessa

I woke up, stretched, and touched warm skin. Sakar's large hands slid around my waist and pulled me toward him. His long, powerful body pressed to mine. He kissed me, long and deep, and I sank into it, in awe that we could do this *every day*.

He was mine. And I was his.

The kiss was all we would do this morning. I pried myself out of his arms with a groan. "Time to get the kids off to school."

He got up, too, stretched, and swung his tail in a circle, as he did every morning upon waking. It was cute. He got dressed. It was still hard for me to remember I wasn't alone in all this. We went downstairs to find Mia still playing video games.

"Go get dressed and brush your teeth," I said to her. "You've got to be out of here in twenty minutes."

The old farmhouse had undergone a well-needed renovation. Everything that had been broken, or barely working, was fixed. It had gotten an electrical upgrade, a new roof, and a nice new paint job. The barns, well, they were amazing. The red barn had been completely redone to accommodate our ship. The one we took back and forth between Earth and Virilia.

My neighbors were still getting used to the idea of having an alien living next door to them, but Sakar won everyone over with his sincerity and ability to lift things without heavy machinery. That went over better than anything else. He'd been over to Mrs. Martina's house to move her refrigerator three times now, and I suspected she just liked watching him flex.

No matter, I was just happy we'd been accepted as the *very* unique family we were. My town was still my town, and my home and land were still mine. The only difference now was that my alien prince was an official ambassador between Earth and Virilia. He had to attend meetings, but they were *good* meetings, which were changing the way Earth behaved toward the alien species we were allied with. Change was coming, and Sakar and I were evidence of that. No one stopped Sakar from coming and going from Earth. It was becoming easier for Virilians to get visitation visas.

"I can't wait to see Axel again," said Mia, as she walked through the house with her toothbrush. "King Virak said we'd be there in time to see the pups born."

"That's the plan," I said, taking a brush to her hair. "So do your best on your vocabulary test today, okay?"

"I will." The girls did a combination of in-school and homeschooling for when we went to Virilia.

So far, it was working well for everyone. The girls were minor celebrities in school, because they got to spend part of their year on the alien planet that spent so much time in the news.

After the girls were on the bus, I slipped into Sakar's arms. "Now, where were we?"

"Making love in our bed?" He raised one dark brow. His tail slid up my thigh.

"I like this plan," I said with a smile. My fingers delved into his thick hair. "We have all week to ourselves before we go to Virilia. We shouldn't wear ourselves out."

His hands slid up my sides. He cupped my ass and pulled my hips tightly against his thick, hard cock. "I think we're both made of stronger stuff," he said with a grin. "We would need far longer than a week for that."

"Hmm." I wrapped my legs around his hips and hung on as he strode, carrying me to the stairs.

"Let's see what you're made of, mate."

"I want you, Sakar," I said before kissing his neck, shoulder, jaw. "On the bed, in the kitchen—everywhere."

"Then you shall have me." His eyes were dark with passion. His pulse beat hard and fast. "I am yours. You are my everything."

I sank into the passionate, loving haze that I never thought I would experience. "And you are mine," I said. "Whatever planet we're on. No matter what."

He laid me on the bed. His hand skimmed over my body, testing the curves he knew well by now. We undressed slowly, luxuriating in the feel of each other. Dipping into the true, deep well that was our love.

Thank you for reading! I hope you enjoyed Sakar and Nessa's story. Please consider leaving a review!

Did you know there are seven books in this series by fabulous sci-fi romance authors? They're all standalone and all amazing!

FROST by Ava Ross
TALIZ by Alana Khan
ZEARN by Rena Marks
BAKI by Ella Maven
SINTA by Honey Phillips
VIXIN by Tana Stone